T O

IN SEARCH OF

GOLD

THROUGH PARTS OF

WILTSHIRE

IN

1808

WRITTEN IN

𝕬 𝔖𝔢𝔯𝔦𝔢𝔰 𝔬𝔣 𝔏𝔢𝔱𝔱𝔢𝔯𝔰

IN WHICH ARE DESCRIBED; A WALK WITH AN *EXECUTIONER,*
A CHANCE ENCOUNTER WITH *REVD. JOSEPH TOWNSEND*
RECTOR OF PEWSEY. AND ALSO *MR. HENRY HUNT* OF UPAVON.
A WITNESS TO THE CONQUERING OF *BUSH BARROW.*
THE PARTICIPATION IN A *CRICKET MATCH* UPON STONEHENGE
DOWN, A DRAMA IN THE SALISBURY *COURT.* A SHORT EXCURSION
WITH *MR. HENRY SHORTO,* ESTEEMED CUTLER OF
SALISBURY, AN ENCOUNTER IN *SALISBURY CATHEDRAL* AND
THE *CONSEQUENCES* THEREOF.

BY

A PEDESTRIAN.

SUTTON VENY:

PUBLISHED BY THE HOBNOB PRESS

2013.

☞ First published in 2013 by The Hobnob Press, 30c Deverill Road Trading Estate, Sutton Veny, Warminster BA12 7BZ

☞ All illustrations are by the author.

☞ British Library Cataloguing in Publication Data: A catalogue record for this book is available from the British Library.
ISBN 978-0-946418-95-4.

☞ Typeset in Bodoni and designed by John Chandler.

Printed in Great Britain by Antony Rowe Ltd.

LETTER TO THE EDITOR

IF IT IS NOT ENTIRELY with the blessing of Mr Henry Chalk that the following pages should now be made available to the expectant public then it is with his indifference for he cannot imagine why any should wish to read of the events that have occurred since the earlier flood of this young Pedestrian Tourist's letters were inadvertently presented as "A Tour in Search of Chalk" and "A Tour in Search of Flint".

I can plainly recall our evening sat before the blazing Radstock coals in the commodious Stourhead Inn where I first promoted the custom of travel, correspondence, embellishment and publication to which my young friend recoiled at the idea of such brazen self-importance. Neither he nor I could foresee the travails and danger that lay in wait for our Pedestrian Tourist and it is only now that a grave tragedy may be laid to rest.

This final volume shall therefore conclude Mr Henry Chalk's pedestrian excursions and as the young author cares not one way or the other then it shall be my own small conceit to dub this work "A Tour in Search of Gold etc etc.."

I wish only happiness for my dear friend and if he never again sets foot upon a country path then let it be through contentment in domestic life for upon this course a destination surely beckons.

Your humble servant
RICHARD FENTON
November 1809

DEDICATION.

DR JOHN CHANDLER
DR MARTIN GREEN

Two doctors, neither of whom would I wish to be examined by but each a generous master in their own fields.

Thursday 1ˢᵗ September 1808

MY DEAR UNCLE,

If you have not yet disowned your errant nephew
then I am indeed the most fortunate and undeserving
of relatives. You will perhaps warm to my plea of
forgiveness when I inform you that I write these words
at my father's desk in the house at Southwark for I have,
at long last, returned home to face my responsibilities.
In truth I cannot convey fully the degree of warmth
expressed by all at Chalk's brewery after my lengthy
absence. I had hoped that I might pass unnoticed to my
old clerk's desk and continue as if nothing at all had
occurred but I have now to occupy my father's office
with my own name inscribed upon the door. As it is
my nature to disrupt, I then caused great consternation
by the cancellation of an order for three vast porter
vats from the Cooper's Company. Mr Gerrity, the
brewery manager, was soon at my door to protest at
this action for he believes that we must keep up with
our competitors in this fashion. Not one week had
passed before I was fully vindicated in my decision
for an identical giant porter barrel at Meux's Horse

Shoe Brewery had, of a sudden, burst its hoops and three workers in the brewhouse were dashed against the walls and killed outright. This is sickening news indeed but it has silenced the clamour for greater volumes of porter than we are safely capable of producing.

You will also recall my account of the digging of the great well in the brewery yard and the hand-wringing that it caused my father, your brother, whilst he was alive. Chalk's Brewery now has the purest water in all London but it is also the hardest water for it is born from the chalk deep beneath the City and as such is not so suitable for the brewing of Porter. I have instead, this last month, visited Burton upon Trent where pale ales are now successfully brewed and for which our harder water is ideally suited. We are but a small concern when compared to our gargantuan neighbours at the Anchor Brewery in old Deadman's Place which now occupies a full nine acres with stabling for 100 horses. From our lowly beginnings as a vinegar factory in Dirty Lane we are spread to three acres with stabling for 30 horses but I proclaim that Chalk's Pale Ale will soon be the talk of all London and indeed I shall eat my snakecatcher's hat if I am to be proved wrong.

Today the bells have rung out in Southwark and all across London in celebration of a victory in Portugal after the defeat of General Junot. I do not understand the complexities of this engagement in the Peninsular but if it assists to end this raging war then there is just cause for such resounding celebration.

I am Sir unable to with-hold the news that I am to meet with Miss Sarah Foster and her brother Robert Foster in Salisbury upon the 10th day of September. I am first to spend some days in the company of Mr William Cunnington for he has invited me to a barrow opening upon the plains near Stonehenge and so Wiltshire is again to be my destination. Mr Gerrity has stated with good humour that he will be glad to see the back of me before I cause yet more disruption here at Southwark. The Chief Clerk, Mr Hooper, who is a kindly man, has I believe been entrusted by my dear friend Mr Richard Fenton to watch over me since my return to Southwark. I am to be cosseted lest my impetuous nature guides me towards some fresh and unforeseen danger for I am then to be passed into the care of Mr William Cunnington and in turn, like some delicate vase, to be received by Mr Robert Foster. Indeed perhaps I am deserving of this watchfulness after my near burial in the flint pit upon the plains of Wiltshire. I should perhaps be more grateful for the concern displayed by my friends and associates as they weave their conspiratorial web but I do feel that I have grown up also as a consequence of my adventures.

I am doubly aware that I have neglected you my dear uncle these past few months and once I have all my affairs in good order then it is time that we should again meet in person after all these passing years.

So it is Sir, with the scent of more adventure and excitement in my nostrils that I am compelled to pick up my pen to write to you for I believe that you understand your nephew better than my poor father ever understood his own son. Here upon my father's desk in a small heart shaped box I have found a gold ring that does not fit even my little finger and it is my mother's wedding ring. Also contained within the box is a golden curl of my mother's hair that mirrors in shape and colour the gold ring when I place them both upon my palm. I am saddened by the sight of the empty box for what is the heart but a box of love?

I will Sir, keep you informed of my progress and I sincerely hope that my correspondence will not impose too much upon your time and patience.

Your tiresome Nephew,
HENRY CHALK.

POSTSCRIPT,
A most curious event has just occurred that shall now cause me to bring forward my plans and to leave London before sunrise. It is as if by the mention of my father that he has now revealed himself before me and I am perhaps able to glimpse his true character for the first time in my life. Before this moment I only ever witnessed his anxiety in business and his buried grief at the death of my mother when I was but seven years old and since that time his

anger would cloud the air and pervade the house whilst I long believed that I was the cause.

Upon the completion of my short note to you a butterfly passed silently through the open window of my father's study and in time settled upon the top shelf of the bookcase. Mrs Harrison the housekeeper, having found the door ajar, entered the study at this same instant and expressed great surprise upon seeing me at my father's desk for I had not before dared to venture into this room since my return to Southwark. Mrs Harrison is a goodly soul and over the last few months has ended our every encounter with the words "..and thanks be to God for your safe return Master Henry." Her flusterings were then directed at the butterfly and she was all for summoning a feather duster to expel the intruder.

I climbed the bookcase step to gain a closer view of the butterfly which had now settled upon the yellowed curl of a piece of paper that protruded from the pages of a book. I carefully lifted the volume from its place with the creature poised and with its colours concealed between closed wings. Mrs Harrison stood with her arms raised in a condition of great anxiety as I slowly descended from the step and she then gasped as the butterfly burst into haphazard flight to display its crisp scarlet and white markings imprinted upon black velvet. Our silent visitor then made a circuit of the room before sensing a draught of air upon which it quickly disappeared leaving me with

book in hand and Mrs Harrison rushing to close the window
lest it should immediately return.

At Mrs Harrison's departure I reopened the window and
studied the spine of the book that I still clutched in my
hand and I found it to be Gulliver's Travels by Jonathon
Swift. Indeed it is a book that I had long meant to read
and only early last year I asked of my father whether he
possessed a copy to which he answered that he did not
and added that I was not of a sufficient age to understand
its irreverence and it would only offend and corrupt. Each
and every transaction with my father was such that his
word was the end of the matter and no further discussion
was required and yet, here in my hands, was this very
same book. I was now made curious by this deceit and I
opened this volume at the place where the sheet of paper
had been inserted and yet it was not the text of the book
that caught my eye but the writing upon this bookmark
for it was in my father's hand. That this folded page was
torn from a notebook or journal I hold no doubt for one
side was covered by his small and neat handwriting that is
very similar to my own and indeed a stranger to both may
not make a distinction between us. Upon the reverse, the
paper was completely covered in unintelligible squiggles
and marks that were, I believe, similar to those used in
the Orient and yet I had no notion that my father could
comprehend such a remote language for indeed he could
barely manage a word of French. I sat in my father's chair

to read and read again the portion of this journal that was written in English. As the tears welled up in my eyes I spent an age staring at the aperture of the open window with a longing for the beautiful butterfly to return so that I might glimpse again its true and bold colours that looked so plain and desiccated with its wings closed up so tight.

My dear uncle, I now enclose a copy of this page of English for it recalls a distant occasion when two young brothers set out from London to Bristol on business and broke their journey near the town of Marlborough in Wiltshire. I am thrown into great confusion for I cannot recognise the father that I knew and instead I see a young man with a spirit that was once akin to my own. Sir, I would dearly wish to hear your recollection of this journey for it warms my heart to read of these exploits and it is indeed a found treasure to match any that may be recovered from the tombs of our ancient ancestors.

I must therefore gather together my pedestrian accoutrements; my hazel thumbstick, my pack and my snakecatcher's hat. I shall take with me the book Gulliver's Travels and also my mother's wedding ring for having picked it up I find that I cannot now relinquish it but I have returned the curl of hair so that it does not remain an empty box. Before dawn I shall depart for Wiltshire and follow in both your footsteps.

A PORTION FROM MY FATHER'S JOURNAL DATED MAY
1782

AFTER BOARDING OUR COACH at the George and Blue
Boar in Holborn we broke our journey at Beckhampton
and walked back upon ourselves to the great mound beside
the Bath road. I was at first greatly vexed with my brother
for he had suddenly demanded this halt in our progress
to Bristol and it is again a challenge to my seniority and
had our father been present then this circumstance would
certainly not have occurred. When questioned he could
not supply a satisfactory explanation to this behaviour and
instead suggested that we were free men and could do as we
pleased. Our luggage was deposited at the Beckhampton
Inn and rather than sit in a crowded parlour to await the
return of my errant brother I decided to follow on behind.
It was indeed a fine afternoon and my own curiosity grew
as I approached Silbury Hill, for that is the name of this
gigantic and mysterious green pudding.

James was seated at the base of the mound for he had
spied my pursuit and insisted that we should make a
wager of one guinea as to who would ascend the hill first
and reach the summit. I felt compelled to establish my
superiority and so together we made a rush upon the hill
and with a deal of tugging and pushing I ensured that I was

to become the eventual victor. James complained bitterly that I had acted unfairly to which I responded that no list of rules had been drawn up and I then demanded my guinea piece whilst fully aware that the wager had not been bound at the outset.

As we caught our breath and lay upon the summit of Silbury Hill the purpose of our journey from Southwark to the bottle-glass factories in Bristol was soon to drift away like down upon the breeze to leave behind two indolent young men enjoying the sweetness of the air.

We were in time joined by a curious Welshman who made the ascent and was keen to attribute this mound to his Cambrian ancestors. James and I had not considered that this giant hill should be of human design at all and if it were so then by all means it should be our own English pyramid. James was swiftly to his feet to take offence and said that the matter could be easily resolved and threw down his coat. By the look of this man's forearms I judged that he was used to heavy labour and was not at all a person to engage in pugilism. One hour before it had not mattered whether the Welsh or the English lay claim to Silbury Hill for we had not yet arrived nor even knew of its existence. Our Cambrian friend ignored James' posturing and wished instead to debate the matter for his eloquence upon this subject was far more persuasive than his forearms could ever be. He had evidently contemplated the matter for many a year and passed this way often when walking between London and Bristol. He is a stoneworker and his name is Mr Edward Williams or indeed Iolo Morganwg. We had no mysterious second names by which to counter these claims or the barest consideration of the ancient activity of the English to redress the balance of the argument and so we lay about on the grass and listened to Mr Williams.

Before departing to continue his pedestrian journey to Bristol, our Welsh stonecutter cast his arm around in all directions to indicate the ancient activity that has occurred hereabouts. Indeed at very close quarters to our elevated position the village of Avebury exists within an enormous entrenchment where vast crude stones have been raised and James queried whether these also were attributed to our friend's Cambrian ancestors. On receiving certain confirmation of this fact James sighed deeply and lay back upon the turf.

After saying farewell to the itinerant Welsh stonecutter my brother informed me that we were dull city dwellers and as we were in England and not Wales then it was beholden upon us to become familiar with these ancient haunts in case we met with another foreigner who availed to tutor us upon our own relics. I could but agree to this action and so we traversed back down the enormous man made hill and spent a fine day discovering all manner of ancient curiosities. We later encountered jumbles of rocks that littered this green sward and did provide the material for the great stone circle in the village of Avebury and also, so we have been informed, the giant stones of Stonehenge. These are called "Sarcen" stones and how they came to be formed only adds to the plethora of mysteries that abound in this quarter of Wiltshire. James raised the question of how these tremendous stones may have been transported from their place of origin to the village of Avebury and indeed to the distant site of Stonehenge. The urge was then upon me to abandon my quest for the investigation of bottle-glass manufacture in Bristol and to make instead a journey upon foot to Stonehenge. I could not however break from the bond of responsibility to my Father for he has finally given sanction to my idea of a bottle glass factory as an annex to Chalk's Brewery and the creation of our own bottled "Superior Stout" to rival any in London and indeed to export far and wide across the globe. Chalk's Brewery must come before any antiquarian ramble and so I urged James to accompany me to the Beckhampton Inn that we may collect our luggage and resume our journey to Bristol. We rushed a decent meal and it was necessary to ride on the outside of the next coach to Bath and then on to Bristol.

....And so ends this fragment of my Father's journal

Friday 2nd September 1808

MY DEAR UNCLE,

This early morning I departed from London upon the
Golden Cross coach where I was surely fortunate to secure
an inside seat. In the darkness we settled together like
chickens in a coup and I soon lolled into a skittish slumber
to join the snuffling chorus of my fellow passengers. As
the earth rotated in union with the grinding wheels dawn
was reached somewhere near Slough and from thereon
loud conversation intruded upon my wandering dreams.
Eventually at the town of Marlborough I decided to abandon
my precious seat, although I had paid to Beckhampton, for
I was keen to feel the earth beneath my feet and begin
life again as a pedestrian tourist. In truth, neither could
I proceed for another minute in the company of a proud
hangman by the name of Mr William Brunskill. There was
not one condemned felon who had escaped the "drop" by
the hand of this boastful executioner upon the gallows
outside Newgate Gaol and each fatal episode was revisited
for the entertainment of his fellow passengers. A pocket
book, produced by Mr Brunskill, prompted the recital of
this morbid litany and after being passed amongst us we

were then informed as to the nature of the leather binding of this small volume for it was indeed a portion of skin from the cadaver of the notorious Owen Haggerty. One fascinated lady passenger was encouraged by the hangman to draw this vile relic across a large wart upon the end of her nose with a certain assurance that this disfigurement would soon be made to vanish entirely by such contact. I can inform you, my dear uncle, that Mr Brunskill is away from his place of work to invest his gallowside manner and tales of finality upon a dying relative in Bristol. After divulging his purpose, Mr Brunskill leant across to wink at me.

"Hope never made a rich man, did it ever Mr Chawk?" Thereafter, and for the remainder of the journey, I tried not to meet the hangman's eye.

The coach finally halted at the Castle Inn which is situated at the western margins of the town of Marlborough. After hastily collecting my pack and thumbstick, I had barely taken my first draught of sweet Wiltshire air when I spied before me a grand curiosity. Placed upon the valley floor and within a stone's throw of the Inn exists a huge mound that was partially concealed under a cloak of vegetation. A brief inspection revealed substantial terracing and it is unlike any Wiltshire barrow that I have yet encountered. I wonder as to the antiquity of this giant heap and confirmed aloud to myself that this could not be Silbury Hill for I have seen Mr William Stukeley's book of

"Abury" where Silbury Hill is shown to stand alone upon open ground. I dutifully began to count my steps around the base of the mound and upon the near completion of this circuit I became fully distracted from my task by the approach of the hangman, Mr William Brunskill.

"Oh my gawd Mr Chawk..what 'ave I done? I've only sent me trunk on to the Beck..summat..Inn. Treat me kind Mr Chawk for I ain't done nuffink like this before."

At first I could not comprehend this circumstance as to why the proud hangman was not aboard the coach that I could now see departing with fresh horses from the yard of the Castle Inn.

"What 'ave I done?" repeated Mr Brunskill as he flapped his hat at a small host of late summer flies that had gathered above his head. "I says to myself, if I is to become a gent'mun then I must do's gent'munly fings and I sees you as a proper young gent'mun Mr Chawk, a proper young gent'mun, but I ain't got no boots I ain't."

I now regretted deeply, whilst aboard the coach, my expounding of the pleasures available to the pedestrian tourist for I knew not the consequence of this idle conversation. I could see no remedy to this situation with the hangman entrusting himself to my company for the journey ahead, until I was able to reunite him with his belongings at the Beckhampton Inn.

I then produced John Cary's map of Wiltshire that is much travel worn but still legible and I gauged that we had a walk of six miles ahead to Silbury Hill and thereafter a short distance on to Beckhampton.

"Wos that then, Mr Chawk?"

I explained that it was a map of the County of Wiltshire and that all pedestrian tourists should be in possession of a map.

"Ooh, then I must gets a map", confirmed the hangman to himself.

At first I thought that if I struck out at a decent pace my already perspiring walking companion would quickly reconsider his hasty decision and return instead to the Castle Inn to await the next coach to Bristol but Mr Brunskill dutifully trotted on behind, whistling as he went, with his short arms dangling at his sides. The afternoon was set fair and we soon crossed the gentle River Kennet by a narrow footbridge where I made a halt. By shading my eyes against the sun, I tried to establish the make up of the stones upon the river bed but I soon became aware that Mr Brunskill was observing my posture closely and he then emulated my stance to the extent of shading his own eyes although he knew not what he observed.

"Very good Mr Chawk, very good indeed".

As I departed from the bridge the hangman paused to make his own observation.

"Look see, an 'orse. A white 'orse up on the 'ill."

With a stumpy finger my uninvited companion eagerly gestured towards the higher slopes of the valley to the South of the town of Marlborough and I looked back with little enthusiasm to observe the figure of a large horse engraved upon the hillside. Whilst turning abruptly to continue on my way I stated that it had surely been created by the removal of the overlying turf to reveal the gleaming chalk that abounds in this County and I could offer no account as to its purpose.

"A chawky 'orse" Mused Mr Brunskill and he then chuckled to himself "Mr Chawk on 'is chawky 'igh 'orse."

No amount of purposeful striding or lengthy pondering was sufficient to dampen the enthusiasm of the hangman for whatever my action, it was deemed to be appropriate to the business of pedestrianism and Mr Brunskill was now my attentive student. We continued by peaceful lanes to the village of Manton where I announced brusquely that we should leave the valley in pursuit of a view with a desire to ascend the Downs that lay to the north of the Bath road. To further bemuse my walking companion, the Downs were made to wait their turn for in a narrow meadow placed between a twist in the river and the turnpike, we there stumbled upon three large recumbent sarcen stones to match in scale those found amongst the outer circuit at Stonehenge. I quickly set to, pacing about the place to inspect the length and breadth of these broad stones and also the degree of workmanship undertaken by the ancient stonemasons. There is also a large pit adjacent to these resting giants that tells of a fierce conflagration not long occurred with broken and blackened fragments of stone at its base.

Mr Brunskill soon found a perch upon one corner of a huge sarcen block where he puffed contentedly on his pipe whilst observing my antics. In my excitement I spoke of the late Mr William Stukeley for he laments the past destruction of the erected sarcen stones that abound in this mysterious land and decries this practice as an "atto de fe". If the stone stands erect then a pit is dug beside it and this stone is then made unstable by further digging. Loose rocks are placed in this execution pit and the condemned stone is then tugged and toppled to crash down upon them and a great fire of wood is started beneath the fallen sarcen. Once a tremendous heat has engulfed the giant, a line is drawn across the rock with cold water and this hissing mark is struck upon with great blacksmith's hammers and wedges are driven in to complete the task.

The hangman considered this statement at length before blowing out a stream of tobacco smoke that drifted steadily between us.

"Straw, Mr Chawk, not wood, straw."

I made a closer inspection of the pit and could now detect some residue of charred straw remaining at its base and confirmed that it would indeed make perfect sense to use straw at a time of harvest when, although still an expense, it was surely more plentiful than firewood.

Mr Brunskill then directed the long stem of his pipe

The Hangman at Devil's Den

towards my feet and shook his head slowly.

"Call's yerself a peddlestring tourist Mr Chawk? You needs the services of a good cobbla'."

I looked down and sure enough my stocking was there for all the world to see as the toe and the sole of my right boot had now parted company. To establish that it would take more than a damaged boot to deter my progress, we crossed the Bath road to explore the Downs.

In time we encountered an arrangement of sarcen lumps where a large capstone rests upon two irregular supporting stones and I have made a brief drawing for you my dear Uncle.

I explained to Mr Brunskill that this was once a tomb

and indeed I had seen others like it in Pembrokeshire, in
South West Wales. Upon receipt of this information my
curious walking companion nodded to himself as he now
added this essential piece to his ever expanding inventory
of prerequisites. Indeed as you well know, my dear uncle,
the complete pedestrian tourist must at all times furnish
the tales of his peregrinations with the casual and liberal
inclusion of such far away places.

"Pem..burr ..oke ..shia", repeated Mr Brunskill "Very
good Mr Chawk, very good indeed."

I peered beneath the capstone with no great expectation
other than to meet the strong aroma of the sheep that had
long sheltered here. Indeed, I was made to start violently,
for the hangman had silently traversed to the opposing
side of the structure and of a sudden forced his round head
through an aperture to bark loudly in my face as if he were
a mad creature.

"Grrrrahh".

In my surprise I clattered my head against the capstone
as I recoiled from the tomb with Mr Brunskill making a low
guttural laugh that became curiously exaggerated by the
partial stone walls within the ruined tomb.

Unsettled by this wild eyed unpredictability I hastened
our retreat from the downs, preferring instead the security
of the busy Bath road but stating that the condition of my
boot now made any further progress an impossibility. With
a growing unease, I stumbled on as best I could with the

hangman trailing close behind me. I wondered whether
all was as it first appeared and my suspicions grew with
every troubled step regarding the purpose of this angel of
death now poised at my shoulder. I have indicated my dear
uncle that my good friends and colleagues have conspired
to ensure my protection to see that I come to no harm for I
have indeed given them good reason with my near burial
in the flint pit behind the Winterslow Hut. There is also
a silent concern that exists only in the expressions and
glances between my adult protectors although I am at a
loss as to be able to identify this lurking danger. I confess
my dear uncle, that I pretend not to notice this clandestine
mollycoddling but the circumstances surrounding the death
of my father are a reoccurring whisper. To leave Southwark
early with a desire to ascend Silbury Hill has laid me bare
to whatever fate has in store and I now found myself alone
in the company of a man who snuffs out life as one would
extinguish a candle. Of a sudden the whistling had ceased
and I had no means by which to gauge the hangman's
proximity behind me. For a shocking moment I felt about
my neck the hands of the executioner who quickly released
his grip to thrust his short arms up further to clamp his
hands across my eyes. As I called out in alarm the flapping
sole of my boot caught a protruding stone causing me to
sprawl upon the grass thereby releasing myself from the
attentions of Mr Brunskill.

"Oh! Mr Chawk, oh my gawd."

The hangman was quick to lend his assistance and soon hauled me upright to set me down upon one of the ubiquitous sarcen blocks that populated the narrow valley in which we now found ourselves.

"There, there, Mr Chawk, you 'as a little rest."

The squat figure of Mr Brunskill sat down a short distance away upon another rock and dangled his shoes above the turf with his round face a picture of reassurance. After a moment he straightened his back and purposefully cleared his throat to break the silence;

"Good young Mr Chawk..I is 'umbly sorry for making you jump n' tumble n' squawk like a parrat. Old Brunskill's been finking about it and it ain't becomin' of one 'oo wishes to be a piddlestain tourist."

I stated that his action had indeed unsettled me for I was not prepared for such antics.

"It's wot they expects o' me Mr Chawk.." exclaimed the hangman with a shrug, "..if I ain't droppin' 'em at Newgate then I is scarin' 'em arf to deaf. It's wot I does."

I could only laugh out loud at this curious disclosure and Mr Brunskill chuckled also as he reignited his pipe.

"Then awl is now well, Mr Chawk?"

I confirmed that all was now well and we settled to look about at our surrounds to find that the grass here in this narrow valley was littered with rock and grazing sheep in equal proportions. There is indeed a similarity between wool and stone when viewed from a distance for it causes the curious illusion of sedentary mutton and shifting geology.

A small bird arrived and flitted from rock to rock until it settled upon one sarcen lump which had the added attraction of a natural sink of water in its pitted surface. Fine tail feathers lengthened this bird twofold and we watched as it bobbed about in its black, white and grey livery but with a scruffy face as if it were an unwashed urchin dressed to be a footman. This little visitor soon fussed in the water and gaily splashed about until it gave a haughty nod in our direction and dashed away in weightless flight as if to mock our heavy earthbound existence.

"'Tis a good day Mr Chawk, a very good day."

I could but agree with the mischievous hangman after now dispelling my foolish doubts regarding his genuine interest.

"I believes that I shall makes a good puddlestrewn tourist Mr Chawk, in time, when I 'as got some boots, a map as you calls it, an' a stick."

I smiled to reassure the hangman that this would indeed be so but privately Sir, I believe that a little restraint may be required if we are not all to jump from our skins when we least expect it.

Upon our departure from the rock strewn valley we took a lift with a carrier whose final destination was the town of Devizes that lies beyond the village of Beckhampton by some ten miles. We first diverted to the small villages of

Lockeridge and West Overton before we finally rounded a corner and there before us rose the wondrous Silbury Hill and my stomach gave a giant leap for, as you well know, it is a truly astonishing sight. Ancient man has demonstrated that nature may be improved upon and that the gentle declivities of the Wiltshire chalklands required, in their estimation, an additional attraction. As the diminutive ant will gather in force to construct an anthill and so a forgotten population has mustered to build a gigantic mound but under whose auspice this work was done makes a riddle to confound even the most diligent antiquarian. Plump Silbury Hill provides an ample target for any fool's bolt and the local wisdom offered by the carrier is that King Sel is buried here resplendent in a suit of gold armour and seated upon his horse. My dear uncle, if our enquiry proceeds no further than the acceptance of this tale then we might call this mound sepulchral and be done with it.

The carrier halted at the base of Silbury Hill and I was fully prepared to pay him a shilling for his trouble but Mr Brunskill would not hear of it and explained that he would now attend to the small business in hand. I was then forcefully encouraged to begin my assault upon Silbury Hill whilst the hangman struck a noble pose and declared his profession to the carrier with his foot firmly aboard the step of the cart to prevent any hasty departure.

"..Deaf...'as bin my life..." I heard the hangman announce cheerfully as I crossed the turnpike with my boot now flapping open like the mouth of a panting dog.

There is a spur of ground that connects Silbury Hill with the adjacent road and I made my tentative approach by hopping upon a worn and narrow trail before this incline had me puffing greatly. I paused to catch my breath and then decided to dispense with my broken boot for it did more to hinder than to help. With my stocking slipping upon these mighty grass slopes I was forced to crawl and tug my way to the summit of Silbury Hill. I confess that a great emptiness then descended upon me for I believe that I expected to find, revealed before me, two young men at liberty lying upon the grass enjoying the late afternoon sun. How ridiculous and impossible is this notion, my dear uncle, to follow with such expectation in my father's footsteps for I shall only ever catch up with him when I am dead? I then made a ponderous circuit of the broad plateau and looked out upon a vast panorama with unseeing eyes, thinking not of the view before me but all the while of my father. After retreating to the comfortable hollow at the centre of the summit of Silbury Hill I took from my pocket the portion of my father's journal that described the scene played out upon this elevated stage over twenty five years ago. I had not read more than one sentence before Mr Brunskill's round head appeared on the horizon and having achieved the summit he staggered wildly, fanning himself with his hat. After his great exertion I thought that the hangman might expire before me as he took a succession of gasping breaths with the displaced phlegm of years gurgling in his chest.

"Mr Chawk…we musts ..'ave a little drink..come ..I 'as got money..on the account of sellin'..an inch of rope that 'ung 'Aggerty..to the lady wiv the fing on 'er nose in the coach..and a twist of 'Olloway's 'air to the country 'Arry . Come, ee's waitin' dahn the 'ill".

Mr Brunskill patted the coins in his purse and indicated for us to now continue on our way with the obliging carrier to the Beckhampton Inn.

"Piddlestrain tourists needs to sluice their gobs… same as any uva cove..'ain't that so Mr Chawk?"

I assured Mr Brunskill that I would soon follow on behind and catch him up at the Inn for I had some observations that I wished to attend to whilst still atop Silbury Hill.

"As you will Mr Chawk, as you will."

I watched as the hangman disappeared from view until all I could see from my hollow was the evening sky with its sparse high clouds now tinged with the golden hue of a retreating sun. I did not return to the reading of the page from my father's journal but instead let my mind wander until I became aware of voices and as I then believed that I would soon have company I hastily raised myself and brushed away the late summer grass from my garments. It was soon apparent that the voices that I could hear came from the sloping fields that lay across the narrow valley where a team of men with great sickles were slicing their way through the ripened corn and I moved to the edge of my giant man made hill to observe this operation. As the corn stalks fell they were gathered up by women with their backs bent to the task and these small bundles were in turn collected and propped together by labouring children into neat shapes and indeed the whole proceeding was conducted in an orderly and constant motion. This murmur of country voices bound together into a low moaning sound as if this tight gathering was but one weary machine moving slowly about the field. The periodic screeching of the sharpening stones across the long blades brought a brief halt to this labour and crooked backs were straightened before the invigorated steel again swept through the cornstalks to set this team into motion once more. Indeed the harvest must be the zenith of all tasks in the agricultural calendar and now entering September the bulk of the prize is surely preserved in the farmyards and I wonder that the late August rain has caused some delay to the collection of these remaining acres.

My thoughts then settled upon Silbury Hill itself and there is a question that returns to me over and again when confronted by the great endeavour of our ancient ancestors; why are they so placed, these raised stones or giant mounds? I believe that we could today emulate our ancient ancestors by building a giant hill or by placing a stone lintel upon two upright sarcens but there is a futility to this action for it is not bound up with the purpose of that forgotten time.

Nor may we plant our modern antiquity in the correct place for we know not why one place is favoured above another. We may argue that Avebury is built at the place where sarcen stones naturally abide and yet Stonehenge lays some twenty miles to the south where only small sarcen stones occur in the fields to disrupt the plough. There is a chasm of knowledge that cannot be obtained by mimicry or indeed by sitting in quiet contemplation upon an anciently made hill for that purpose is now lost and it shall not reveal itself.

Wisdom has not been gained by my clambering to the top of Silbury Hill and I am become overly sour in venting my frustration upon the study of our antiquities. Indeed I now acknowledge that it was my father, or the pursuit of a relic of his once youthful character that has brought me to this place and the one mystery shall only compound the other.

Today the glorious sight of Silbury Hill signals the blowing of the post-horn of the west bound stage upon the Bath road to inform of their approach to the respective Inns of Beckhampton. Just such a horn drew me from my reverie and so I began my slow descent to retrieve on the way my damaged boot.

At the Beckhampton Inn I was greeted with courtesy by the landlord and indeed my arrival had been expected for the celebrated principal hangman at Newgate Gaol had spoken very kindly of his new young friend. I enquired as to where I might now find Mr Brunskill and I felt a curious regret at the news that this same gentleman had just this minute departed for Bristol. I was taken aback when the landlord returned my thumbstick for my walking companion had left it for me to collect and I knew not that I had mislaid it. I afforded myself a smile as I imagined the swaggering arrival at the inn of this novice pedestrian tourist, brandishing my thumbsick. I have perhaps acted unfairly in my dealings with the hangman and it appears as though he could wait no longer before continuing on his journey to comfort his dying relation. The landlord then produced a short portion of frayed rope and announced proudly that it had hung the evil Holloway and he excused himself to display this morbid relic to his other guests.

It is a problem at this busy Inn to find a spare table corner upon which to write for everywhere is jostling, exasperation and impatience and I wonder how many travellers are expected to share a room and a bed in this place. A cobbler will attend to the repair of my boot in the morning and I must abide here at the Beckhampton Inn until his work is done.

Your confused but ever faithful Nephew,
HENRY CHALK.

Saturday 3rd September 1808

MY DEAR UNCLE,

The day here at Beckhampton marches on without me for I
am thwarted by the tardy cobbler as he deigns to keep me
waiting and I am helpless without his attention to my boot.
I have suffered a wretched night also as I have shared a bed
with a seven foot giant who ensured that the trench in the
centre of the mattress was his domain and my paltry share
was but the sloping outer regions. The covers were also
largely employed in the shrouding of this Man Mountain
with only the flimsiest of sheet corners remaining for my
comfort despite my constant gripping and tugging. Indeed
a mountain is an inanimate thing so perhaps a volcano
might better describe my bedfellow. During our nocturnal
association we barely exchanged one word but at the
breakfast table this same huge gentleman, observing the
arrangement of my boiled egg in its cup, then remarked;

"Sir, I see that you are a Big-Endian, perhaps we
should go to war over it?"

Indeed it was true for his own egg was positioned in
the opposing manner to clearly demonstrate his allegiance
to the Emperor of Lilliput. To propose that such minor

issues can lead to war is preposterous, but I believe that
the author of Gulliver's Travels is of the opinion that the
human race is not to be found wanting in that regard. Being
unable to establish any common ground throughout the
night we could now at least be reconciled in our admiration
of Mr Swift's fine book and discuss the various merits of
"Gulliver's Travels". As a consequence of my conversation
with Mr Little, the name of this "Quinbus Flestrin", I am
now greatly informed as to the sly satire that the author
has concocted for I knew not that the squabbles between
Lilliput and Blefuscu referred to our own longstanding
conflict with our troublesome neighbour France.

My gigantic bedfellow lowered his voice as he leant
across the parlour table:

"You have encountered "A Modest Proposal", Mr
Swift's most odious satire..?"

With my mouth full I shook my head to indicate that I
had not.

"..A Modest Proposal For Preventing The Children Of
Poor People In Ireland From Being A Burden To Their
Parents.."

This gentleman made no further explanation other than
to nod grimly before dipping his egg and lowering the
dripping finger of toast into his mouth, tearing and chewing
slowly whilst observing me through wide bloodshot eyes.
At this display of provocative mastication I near choked
on my food and protested that this was indeed an outrage,

if I had interpreted his meaning correctly, and it was not at all a modest proposal.

"Indeed Sir, it is a moral outrage that the author, who is himself of impecunious Irish origins, then turns upon the ruling government. It is satire at its most effective."

Of a sudden I held no desire to complete my own breakfast and so I bid the enormous Mr Little a good morning and thanked him also for his illuminating instruction.

I have now taken a moment to consider that in six days time I shall be reunited with Miss Sarah Foster for it seems an eternity since our first and indeed our only meeting at Hindon on October last. Against my breast I have one of a pair of silver mounted flint hearts that were carefully manufactured in the workshops of Mr Henry Shorto of Salisbury. Flint is cold against the skin and as a consequence I can feel its presence in each and every waking moment. I confess that I had not considered this effect at the outset and did not wish such discomfort upon Miss Sarah Foster but she mocks my concern. In her letters that are by necessity written by her amanuensis, Mr Robert Foster, she states that she wears her gift always and only removes it if there is cause to make a spark for a fire or to skin a rabbit. Indeed which other precious stone may be so useful and I am always greatly mollified by the fondling of my flint heart that hangs upon its silver chain.

In this hiatus there is perhaps an opportunity now to

inform you of the events that occurred after my departure from the Winterslow Hut for I have again been negligent in my correspondence to you my dear uncle. Is it not all or nothing with your errant nephew? I was still much confused after a blow to the head that I received as a consequence of my own foolishness in returning to the flint pit during the great storm. Mr Fenton has recounted to me how I attempted to depart upon my own from the Winterslow Hut but was found collapsed and insensible at the foot of the stairs. I wonder at the patience of my dear friends and also at the generosity of Sir Richard Colt Hoare in permitting my convalescence at Stourhead. In due course the Baronet, in the company of Mr Fenton, then departed for a further tour of Wales and in the ensuing calm I was able to draft a small volume that I flatter myself may one day appear upon the shelves of the Baronet's great library. It will, in part, repay the dept of gratitude that I hold for Sir Richard Colt Hoare for there is as yet no book written on the purposefulness of flint.

Manufactured flint tools and their essential use in everyday life before the common availability of metal by the ancient people of South Wiltshire with an investigation into the likely sources of flint of the finest quality.

Or,
Life before the knife and fork

By

A Pedestrian

I was not to be left unattended at Stourhead and cherished greatly the visits of Mr Philip Crocker who is the surveyor entrusted to the task of compiling detailed maps of South Wiltshire upon which each barrow, camp, British village or standing stone shall be charted. As a skilled draughtsman Mr Crocker has also to draw every drinking vessel, bead, brooch, lance, buckle, knife, battle axe and bodkin retrieved from the barrows to illuminate the Baronet's great work called "Ancient Wiltshire". After explaining his many duties I then shared my modest notions of an investigation into the simple flint tools of the ancient common-folk for whom there are no raised barrows. Flint shall not decay and the scatterings of a remote stone industry may still be found amongst the plough soil today. I explained that I had found crude tools for scraping the fat from a hide, sharp blades to cut, points for piercing leather and all in the vicinity of Stourhead whilst I walked the fields during my convalescence. A discreet visit to the game larder enabled me to test my theories and the flint scraper, which is perhaps the most ubiquitous of the finished tools to be found in the soil, shall gather up and collect the animal fat whilst not puncturing the valuable skin.

"The ancient past is indeed under our very nose Henry

for we have been distracted by the chattels of the kings and
queens. Perhaps these clusters of simple tools and chipped
flint indicate where the common habitations once stood?"

Mr Crocker cheerfully toasted me with a glass of sack
and declared his support for this most worthy undertaking;

"To Mr Henry Chalk ..in his search for the shadows cast
in the soil by the ancient subjects of a forgotten king."

We both laughed openly at this exchange which I take
to be the signs of a burgeoning friendship.

I shall now put down my pen and again join Lemuel
Gulliver upon his travels for I now better understand the
satire of this fine book and it is a comfort to know that my
father once turned these very same pages.

*

My plans are profoundly altered and Avebury must
remain idle and unexplored. I am embarked upon a
journey that my father once contemplated before the bond
of responsibility to his own father and to Chalk's Brewery
determined that he should reject such distractions. Sir
you will have surmised by now that my destination is
Stonehenge and I am resigned to the fact that I will not
discover my father on the way. Indeed I now smile at my
own vain expectation that by some inexplicable means he
should have awaited my arrival atop Silbury Hill.

Safe in the knowledge that I am no Pennant, Warner

or Gilpin, it is not my intention to leave a trail of ink for others to follow but I can report that I am in or near the village of Marden, if I am reading Mr Cary's map correctly. I have before me yet another man made hill that I shall soon attempt to record once I exchange my pen for a pencil. I hope in time to explain the circumstances of my repaired boot and to then praise the soaring profiles and swooping declivities of the high chalklands that lie to the South of Silbury Hill. There is also an extraordinary piece of flint retrieved from the sandy soils of this pleasant vale that requires explanation but such are the circumstances of a most unusual encounter, not long occurred, that all of the above must wait their turn.

My dear uncle, if you will consider a south bound pedestrian tourist now into his stride but ever susceptible to distraction and a giant cleric, brim full of purpose, pacing eastwards along the bank of a newly constructed canal then surely serendipity will cause their paths to cross. I can inform you that these two beings did not collide and it was but curiosity on my part that sufficiently delayed my progress as I gazed down upon the idle waters of the canal from a fine new bridge and only then observed the huge gentleman ambling along the towpath towards me.

"Leaks, leaks and springs." Announced the clergyman as he grew ever larger and then mounted the bridge with hand outstretched.

"Reverend Joseph Townsend of Pewsey. I inspect our

portion of the Kennet and Avon canal weekly for leakages between the towns of Devizes and Pewsey."

Before the act of wrapping his great hand around my own to grip and then shake it with some force, I observed curious ink characters written upon each fingernail and my face surely betrayed some puzzlement for an explanation was immediately forthcoming.

"Ah, you are familiar with Sanskrit? I propose that there is but one original language from which all others are derived but I must first explore these remote scripts. It is a means by which to learn for it is the very nature of fingers to remain visible at all times of the day."

I finally introduced myself to this colossus who I could now see at close quarters was indeed an elderly gentleman although his gait and motion were a country mile from any apparent infirmity. He possessed a great domed brow and a penetrating gaze that quite made me falter as I explained my own purpose which grew more insignificant with each word uttered. To lend gravitas to my tale I then seized upon the plight of the common labourer for I had been greatly troubled by their abject appearance which is indeed the truth. As I passed from the high chalk lands and entered this level and sandy vale I had witnessed the gleaners at their work. These are teams of women and children who scour the brushed golden stubble for any remaining ears of corn at the conclusion of the harvest. Indeed harvesting and its aftermath is hard labour and it is no wonder that the country folk are bent and crooked of gait. Many are also gaunt faced and it is a crime that they are not better nourished when the production of victuals lies at the heart of their labour and a great deal of money shall, in the months ahead, be exchanged at the corn market. Thinking in part of Chalk's Brewery, I concluded by stating that all business requires labour but you do not underfeed your horse for it shall not have the strength to pull the dray, cart or indeed the plough and therefore I could not comprehend why the common labourers were treated so.

I was soon informed that the poor must exercise themselves in all manner of gainful work and the desire to eat shall sweeten even the severest labour.

"Mr Chalk, the poor cannot throw themselves upon the mercy of the Parish and must instead help themselves. No man should seek assistance unless he has exhausted all means within his own power and it is the Poor Laws that are at fault for they only perpetuate the problem and must be reformed without delay."

The clergyman shook his enormous head with his great brow rippled in consternation;

"The population will only exceed its natural bounds and charity without limits shall but increase the population and bring about a greater distress and dissipation."

I was now aghast for I detected not a trace of compassion for the common labourer and stated brazenly that I found these views to be most un-Christian.

At this the giant Cleric loomed towards me and I drew back to the parapet of the bridge. I was now entreated to a simple parable by which to demonstrate the struggles of mankind and a natural order from which the human race was not immune.

"Young Sir, if you will imagine a south sea island.. you have read Robinson Crusoe? Good. Well please dispense with Robinson and Man Friday for we require an uninhabited place save for a herd of goats that roam freely and their numbers increase for it is a verdant place with plenty for the goats to feed upon. One day a greyhound and a bitch are washed ashore.."

The Reverend Joseph Townsend held up his great hand to prevent the questioning of these circumstances.

"..the dogs breed and feed upon the goat population and at first there is sufficient for both the goats and their predators but in time Mr Chalk, the dogs become more abundant and the goats take to the mountains to ensure their survival for the dogs cannot follow upon the steepest rocks and enter these craggy places. It is only the strongest goats that will survive this terrain and as a consequence it is only the fittest dogs that will still catch the goats and so a balance is met. The weakest of both species shall not survive and so a strong race of goats and greyhounds will populate the island."

The clergyman drew his inky fingers together and smiled benignly with the presentation of this gift of logic that surely reduced the human race to nothing better than a struggle amongst animals. My thoughts returned to the circumstances of my breakfast at the Beckhampton Inn when in the company of another giant I was informed of Mr Jonathon Swift's most lacerating satire. Before uttering my parting denouement I carefully extricated myself from between the parapet of the bridge and the towering presence of the Rector of Pewsey.

"With respect I find yours a most Immodest Proposal and had Mr Swift concocted it then he would feel justly pleased with himself. Good day Sir."

As I scuttled from the bridge, with all the while keeping an eye behind me, the Reverend Joseph Townsend turned abruptly about and uttered not one word but I could feel his hard stare until I was hidden from view.

My dear uncle, I am a poor reporter of useful information and had our discourse taken a different turn then I would surely be able to elucidate fully upon the exact progress of the new Kennet and Avon canal. It is indeed a bold and expensive venture and transportation between the cities of Bristol and London shall be greatly improved with benefits also to the many smaller towns and villages along the way. Earlier this year I suggested in all seriousness to Mr Gerrity, our brewery manager, that we should consider the establishment of tied houses beyond the environs of London and this notion was spurred on by my reading with interest about the new Kennet and Avon canal. I firmly

believed that we should seize the opportunity presented
by the canal before our competitors do so in our stead but
Mr Gerrity was not to be so easily persuaded and stated
that we should consider the great cost of acquiring the
necessary property and also the very slow turn around of
the casks. A further obstacle was the necessity for regular
inspections of the beer by our collecting clerks and with
my enthusiasm truly dampened I conceded that Chalk's
Golden Pale Ale in bottle must be our sole new venture. I
now make a silent vow that Chalk's beer shall one day pass
under the new bridge albeit in glass rather than wood.

No water had visibly leaked from the canal during
my curious encounter but a valuable portion of time
had ebbed from the day and my fleet footed departure
was indeed justified in preserving the daylight hours for
the business of pedestrianism. (Sir, as you will know by
now pedestrianism also embraces feverish scribbling,
amateurish drawing, idling, dreaming and disturbing the
common order of places on the way.)

Here in the village of Marden stands the third enormous
man made hill that I have witnessed in this most curious
quarter of Wiltshire and indeed it is a land to rival any
visited by Lemuel Gulliver. The mound is sorely damaged
as if a giant had spooned out its interior and destroyed
the form of this vast upturned pudding. It is a place of
great mounds, outlandish giants and giant white horses
and I have named it Gorabhumlor. Perhaps my father was

justified in expressing his caution as to the effects of my reading Mr Swift's extraordinary book when not yet fully grown to adulthood.

*

The Hatfield Barrow

Sunday morning

MY DEAR UNCLE,

I have a tale to tell that will very soon make you cradle your head in despair at your avuncular association with this pedestrian tourist for he is surely unrivalled in disturbing the common order of people and places. Perhaps there is also a book that should be penned on how flint shall cause a great deal of trouble in the hands of one Henry Chalk for there are chapters already writ and I will now contribute further to this record of irresponsible behaviour. From my position beside the river Avon I can hear the peeling of the church bells from up and down this broad valley for the sound travels well upon the water. I shall write and then rest a while for I have only slept fitfully since my arrival in Wiltshire.

I resume my tale in the village of Marden where there exists a fine display of ancient activity for in addition to the enormous man made hill there is a vast encompassing bank with a broad internal ditch and the winding river concludes the southern boundary of this earthwork. A walk about the village of Marden has revealed that a number of weighty sarcen blocks have been secreted about the place as the church tower sits upon a nest of these alien rocks perhaps to prevent it from sinking into this sandy vale and at the mill the meandering river has large sarcen revetments set into these soft and vulnerable banks. I have today neglected the considerable ancient works about the village of Avebury but I have before studied Mr William Stukeley's fine book dedicated to the antiquities of that place and his illustrations ably depict that a large population of gargantuan sarcen stones are stationed within its own circular enclosure. I am left to wonder whether modern man has prospered by the labours of his ancient ancestors here in this small village for may not these most useful pieces once have adorned this giant enclosure at Marden for they were surely hauled from the sarcen fields that lie to the west of the town of Marlborough? It is indeed a considerable distance from their place of origin but ancient man has already proved his tenacity in this regard by moving these same pieces across Salisbury Plain to Stonehenge and Marden is but half that distance according to Mr John Cary's map of Wiltshire.

As you may establish from my drawing the huge mound has suffered in recent times and I fear that there may soon be a level field where a great mystery once stood, if it is now the farmers will. I sincerely hope that this work was not undertaken in the name of antiquarian curiosity for reparation should rightly follow such intrusive investigation.

In time I left behind this gentle sandy vale and with the climbing of a long escarpment found myself upon the vast and elevated hub of chalk that is Salisbury Plain. I have been informed before that many a traveller has become lost upon the great plain and so it was with a degree of timidity that I chose to walk its periphery and thereby kept a reassuring view across the Avon Valley.

The sheep flocks are numerous and the shepherds are keen to seek company upon their lonely vigil and I have established that the great sheep fairs are soon to be held about South Wiltshire and so a greater massing of these flocks is to be expected in the following days. The sheep shall have their say and save for a gaggle of aggrieved geese these creatures are surely the most vociferous of all livestock for the contagion of a single bleat of alarm shall spread quickly to become an infuriating cacophony. It is indeed little wonder that the shepherds themselves are wild eyed and askew in their manner and cling to a passing stranger like a drowning man to a bobbing barrel.

On these elevated fringes of high chalkland I encountered the very last throes of harvest for I was drawn to investigate a large earthwork called Casterly Intrenchment upon John Cary's map and the internal acres were already turned to a golden stubble save for a scruffy twist of standing corn. The large band of harvesters were now engaged in song and good natured exchanges whilst reclining in the outer ditch and thus in their sunken position did not witness my arrival. Amidst this broad expanse of stubble a huge cloud of identical birds were engaged in their own act of gleaning and I observed as they traversed these cropped acres in a great rolling wave with those at the back leapfrogging to the fore until this great twisting black swarm departed for a neighbouring field. A good number of stooks of corn lay about awaiting collection amongst which were strewn the harvesters tools and I picked up a sickle to feel its weight in my hand. It appeared negligent not to complete the final act of harvest when all about had been cleared and remembering the piece of fashioned flint that I had earlier in the day gleaned from the sandy soils of the vale the opportunity now presented itself to test the keenness of this long blade. From end to end I gauge that it measures in excess of five inches and I shall not hesitate to proclaim it a broad blade for the greatest attention has been given by its maker to fashion the long convex curve of its cutting edge. The most perplexing aspect of this piece is that it glistens along this finely made edge and I have never before witnessed such ancient magic. After removing my pack I gripped firmly the sole remaining clump of standing corn to make it taught and then ripped at the foot of the

The Flint Sickle

plant with my flint and indeed I had some success in severing the stalks one at a time. I then held the piece with a straight finger supporting from behind on the opposing blunted edge and slashed at the remaining standing corn and found this a better means by which to operate with this ancient tool. As I stood amongst the stubbles with the final cut of the annual harvest gathered in the crook of my arm I wondered whether this was the true purpose of this crafted flint and that it was instead a crude sickle rather than a knife as I first thought and I had now fortuitously put the piece to its rightful use. I imagined it set in a cleft of wood for a handle and I also wonder that the glossy polishing of the cutting edge may have been caused by its repeated contact with the ripened corn stalks if indeed ancient man grew corn as we do today.

As I juggled with these perplexing issues I was spotted by the harvesters who to a man, woman and child quickly scampered from their sunny ditch to surround me in large number and the remnants of severed corn and also the flint piece were then hastily snatched from my person. By the look of anger and consternation upon these country faces I feared that I may now be dealt with harshly for the crowd of harvesters jostled and jeered about me whilst I knew not the cause of their grievance. A young woman broke free of the melee and held aloft the severed clump of cornstalks whereupon the throng of rustic voices called out as one;

"A neck, a neck we do 'ave un."

At the conclusion of this curious chant a great cheer was made but this distraction was short lived and a labourer with a dark and bristling beard turned and pushed me firmly to the ground and then spat upon his hands as if we were now to engage in a bout of pugilism. As he gestured again for me to stand I decided to remain amongst the stubbles whilst another call went up from the harvesters;

"Yerr's the Squire, the Squire's coom."

The belligerent mood amongst the harvesters now turned to panic as fifty or more of the labourers scampered amongst the remaining stooks of corn to collect their scattered tools. The galloping hooves of the Squire's mount resounded thunderously upon the dense chalk mass of the Plain as if it were not a man at all but instead a giant that was fast approaching. Wide eyed and ashen faced the bearded man stood with some reluctance to the fore of the cowering harvesters and removed his hat as the rider pulled up before him. The Squire glowered down upon the meek assemblage and his stentorian voice boomed out across Casterly Intrenchment.

"You bring shame to Widdington. Never in my father's day were we the last farm to bring in the harvest. We shall long hear the gibes up and down the valley. Your father was never late with the contract when he was harvest lord. We shall be a disgrace to both our father's names. Explain yourself man?"

The bearded labourer stammered that they had suffered badly with the weather but his excuses were soon disregarded by the mounted Squire.

"It is the same for all, the same for all…and who is that upon the ground?"

The Squire coaxed his horse to encircle the harvesters to examine this stranger in their midst. The gathering now recovered their voice and all clamoured together to describe the part I had to play in the disruption of the final act of harvest as if I were now in some way to be blamed for the protracted lateness of the whole.

"Ee did cut the neck, Zquire zur.. with thic vlint."

The Squire looked down upon me and his voice again boomed forth;

"What is your name Sir and why are you cowering amongst the stubbles?"

I hastily stood and gave my name but was interrupted from any further explanation by the harvest lord in his attempt to regain some pride before the gang of harvesters.

"Oi did push un thur zur,"

"Aha, and a wish to bloody his nose I'll wager? Well get to it man. Mr Chalk, defend yourself."

With the arrival of the booming Squire I thought my prospects improved but he now appeared as keen as any to witness a fight and as I made no move to prepare for battle, the Squire drew closer with his horse.

"Are you a man or a boy?"

I declared that I was a traveller who did not wish to fight at all and apologised wholeheartedly for my interference with the last rites of the annual harvest, for I knew not that I had done wrong.

"It is done Sir, for whatever the reason and now cannot be undone."

At this impasse the Squire frowned and the harvesters muttered amongst themselves whilst a wagon lumbered slowly towards us bedecked with ribbons.

"There are two things that must now occur.." broadcast the mounted Squire "..if there is to be no honour established. You Sir, must firstly pay a generous largesse toward the harvest celebrations to assuage for your interference here today."

The harvesters nodded vigorously and the harvest lord led a loud cheer at this welcome proposal.

"Secondly.." Announced the Squire, effortlessly silencing the excitable group with an extraordinary vocal power ".. he who cuts the neck must sit at the table for our celebration of the harvest, for that is the custom. Mr Chalk, like it or not, you shall be joining us this evening. It is a situation of your own making."

The harvesters were audibly less keen on this second condition but had to concede the correctness of the Squire's ruling. The paying of the largesse was to be undertaken immediately and I knew not what sum was appropriate and looked to the Squire for guidance.

"It is a negotiation to be conducted between the passing stranger and the harvest lord. Mr Chalk you have blindly stumbled upon a custom that is centuries old."

I duly paid my largesse and my disadvantage was surely exploited by the emboldened harvest lord. The wagon now arrived carrying the very young and the very old to welcome home the harvesters and to collect the final stooks of corn. The all important "neck" was received aboard with great reverence and after further cheering I was then invited to accompany the final journey of harvest from field to farmyard. The Squire galloped on ahead and there was a deal of muttered explanation to the elders who had just arrived and ensuing scowls at this young stranger in their midst. I walked behind the laden wagon in silence wishing again that I had given more thought to my actions. A flask was thrust towards me by a young labourer which proved to contain cider and I was indeed glad to quench my thirst. There was an expectant mood amongst the harvesters with the knowledge that a feast lay ahead and neither a berating by the Squire at the lateness of the harvest or indeed my interference could subdue the weary labourers who sang with gusto under the open skies of Salisbury Plain.

I shall now rest a while before continuing on my way and in due course I promise to conclude the account of the harvest celebrations.

*

Sunday evening

My dear Uncle,

I am now comfortably installed at the George Inn in Amesbury with pen in hand whilst Mr John Fenton is playing a pleasing welsh air upon his flute before the open window in the next room. There is still much to report and I am gratified also that there appears to be some distance between Beckhampton and Amesbury upon Mr John Cary's map for Mr John Fenton duly raised an eyebrow upon my arrival when I demonstrated the full span of my finger and thumb between these two places.

"Henry, your appetite for itinerancy is admirable but I understood that that you were to travel directly from Southwark to Amesbury?"

I explained that I had found a portion of a diary or notebook in my father's hand that described an unscheduled visit to Silbury Hill in the year 1782 when he and his brother James, my uncle, were travelling to Bristol upon business and it was indeed a flight of fancy on my part that caused me to follow in their footsteps. I was then scolded for behaving without responsibility and I am now bemused by this new concern for I have experienced before John Fenton's propensity for raillery. I am, however, pleased to be reunited with Mr Richard Fenton's eldest son who has informed me that he is still attempting to straighten his back after a lengthy journey from Pembrokeshire.

"I calculate that I have aged ten years in that wretched coach whilst you have a brightness in your eyes that speaks only of pleasurable travel. I believe that I must accompany you Mr Henry Chalk on one of your pedestrian excursions."

With this declaration John picked up my thumbstick and with a crooked back and ancient voice to match he embarked upon a circuit of the parlour tapping at the flagstones.

"I am old and cannot see..is young Chalk ahead of me?"

I know not whether this desire is genuine but I hold no doubt that Mr John Fenton shall require company this evening and so I must continue with my account of the final gathering of the harvest upon the eastern fringes of Salisbury Plain.

The destination for our noisy entourage was Widdington Farm which nestled comfortably in a valley below Casterly Intrenchment. A number of rotund corn ricks were already constructed in the farm yard and the scene was made gay with ribbons and green garlands. A large barn was to be the setting for the harvest supper and I clung sheepishly to the shadows of a broad elm tree whilst the final preparations were being conducted. The harvesters, who were not engaged in the building and thatching of the final rick, sat about in clusters drinking cider and singing rounds whilst the children played and danced.

The Squire now emerged from the farmhouse where he had paid a visit to the farmer who had been made absent from the proceedings as he was laid abed with a broken bone in his leg.

After inspecting the great bulging ricks, the Squire spied my attempted concealment in the shadows of the great tree and marched across the farmyard to stand before me with hands on hips.

"I recall Mr Chalk that I have not yet introduced myself. I Sir, am Henry Hunt."

I had never before heard mention of this gentleman's name and simply offered my hand to be shaken but he at first ignored this gesture for he appeared bemused by my lack of surprise at his disclosure.

"Then you are not a gossip monger and as such shall form no opinion other than by your own judgement of the man that stands before you?"

"Indeed I shall not Sir", I replied.

I dared not ask the nature of such notoriety that should arm my prejudice and I explained instead that I was a pedestrian tourist who was to meet shortly with Mr William Cunnington and his family upon Stonehenge Down where a further campaign of barrow opening was due to commence. I explained that under the patronage of Sir Richard Colt Hoare a great deal of antiquarian investigation has already been undertaken to assist with this same nobleman's forthcoming publication that is to be titled "Ancient Wiltshire". I felt certain that these associations might help my cause in the eyes of the Squire but he was quick to undermine such presumptions.

"A fine distraction, I must say, from the important matters of the day. He made a negligent High Sheriff, vanishing into the wastes of Wales, when his duties were plainly at home in Wiltshire upon matters of national importance."

Surprised as I was by this accusation, there was no requirement for me to question this circumstance as Mr Henry Hunt gave a voluble and lengthy account of how he once addressed a public meeting of freeholders in Devizes to protest at the conduct of Lord Melville, who was then the Treasurer of the Navy. Lord Melville was implicated in

defrauding the public of the monies entrusted to his position
and all across the kingdom public meetings were being held
calling for a full enquiry into the matter. "Getting wind of
the gathering storm the High Sheriff, your Sir Richard Colt
Hoare, was nowhere to be found and I proposed a vote of
censure upon such irresponsible conduct. Being young in
politics at the time I was prevailed upon to withdraw my vote
after receiving an apology. It was to be my first entry into
public life Mr Chalk and I have since gained many friends
and enemies along the way and amongst the latter shall sit
the bloodsucking landowners of this County and those two
corrupt factions the Whigs and the Tories. Amongst the
former I count the oppressed and our Radical Reformers
and indeed Mr William Cobbett for he frequently reports
my various successes in his Political Register."

I had not heard of Mr Cobbett nor his publication
and indeed my dear uncle you will know me to be one
whose thoughts and aspirations are directed toward the
past and I know little of political life and so I remained
silent as Mr Hunt puffed out his chest and gave vent to his
accomplishments.

Eventually he asked after my own affairs whereupon I
made brief reference to Chalk's Brewery which sent this
splenetic gentleman into a rage upon the dishonesty of
brewers. He then boomed forth that his business venture
in Bristol was recently made bankrupt where in attempting
to brew fine and unadulterated beer he found the entire

business racked with dishonesty, malpractice and skimping against which no honest man could compete.

"I suggest Sir that your business is no different."

My bile quickly rose to firmly defend Chalk's Brewery and I told this gentleman that the principals to which he claimed to adhere were identical to our own; hops and barley malt of the finest quality and indeed the purest water in all London from the new well that plunges six hundred feet below the streets of Southwark. I concluded that our family had been respected and conscientious brewers and that my father had proudly adhered to this tradition and I too, in my tenure, would now strive to do the same.

Mr Hunt nodded with approval, perhaps as much at my heartfelt and stout defence as at the description of our methods.

The convivial atmosphere in the farmyard was at odds with our heated exchanges and despite my apparent obligation to remain at the harvest celebration, I was to be no prisoner and would now challenge any that prevented my departure such was my anger. I had heard more than enough from the self regarding Squire and was about to depart when a young maid with late summer flowers in her hair approached with two mugs of cider and offered them to Mr Hunt and myself. As I thanked the maid the Squire looked at me quizzically.

"Mr Chalk, am I to understand that you have succeeded your Father in the running of your business?"

I was taken aback at this enquiry but confirmed that my father had indeed died not eighteen months ago, an event which had projected me with some reluctance to face up to my responsibilities.

"Then please accept my sympathies at your loss Mr Chalk for you are still young."

The Squire then disclosed that it was the memory of his own father that caused him to make his infrequent returns to Widdington Farm for Mr Thomas Hunt had died eleven years ago and had been buried upon the eve of the "Harvest Home", the name given to this end of harvest celebration. Despite this gentleman's wind and bluster I now envy the fact that father and son grew up in accord and that Mr Hunt was at his father's side when he took his final breath and how I wish with all my heart that my own circumstance were the same. For all his propensity to enjoy the sound of his own booming voice, Mr Hunt listened to the tale of my abrupt departure from Southwark after the fortuitous finding of the page written in my own father's hand which led in turn to my divulging the tragic circumstances of his death.

"Then Mr Chalk we have found a common purpose for is it not our fathers that have brought us here today? We must now make a toast to their memory. I cannot assist with your perplexing tale and I was all for boxing your ears for disturbing the harvesters but now let all be forgotten. Our dear fathers!"

We both held a tear in our eyes as we raised our pots after which Mr Henry Hunt clapped me heartily on the back.

"Mr Chalk, you still appear bewildered by your presence here at Widdington. I should explain that the last sheaf of standing corn from the annual harvest is treated with great reverence by the harvesters and it has always been so. It is believed that the spirit of the harvest has retreated to those remaining stalks and such is their superstition that no man wishes to be responsible for this final act of severance or indeed meddle with the spirit for fear of endangering future yields. Despite the upheaval you have caused, and I do not wish to hear the reasons why, you have at least spared them this dread task and although none shall speak of it, to a man, woman and child they are silently relieved and of course have financially prospered by your actions. Sir, you may be at your ease this evening and no person here shall display any grievance towards you."

I felt a deal better after Mr Hunt's assurances and he now of a sudden excused himself to confront the parson who had just arrived in Widdington farmyard.

"Lo, it is the hungry parson."

Upon witnessing the Squire standing before him, the alarmed churchman briskly turned about his phaeton and departed from the harvest celebrations with the roar of Mr Henry Hunt's laughter ringing in his ears. Having emerged from the shadows to join the celebration I and all present were now stricken and frozen in silence as the Squire's laughter faded and he turned to scowl at the harvesters.

"He is a parasite, you shall not clap eyes upon him from one year to the next for he lives not in Upavon and serves no person but himself. These swinging parsons must be made to lower their tithes, the landlords to lower their rents to the farmers and you must all receive a fair wage. To this end, nothing short of radical reform is required. Universal suffrage, freedom and free speech shall be denied you until there are honourable and independent men in government. I am such a man. I am a friend to the poor."

Mr Henry Hunt now stood alone in the centre of the farmyard as his booming pledge resounded about the valley causing the roosting colony of large black birds atop the giant elm to take to the sky and the lame farmer to hastily arise and close his bedroom window. We may be there still, every man, woman and child as if we were ourselves a cast of anxious faces captured in a painting with the athletic figure of Mr Henry Hunt bestriding all at its centre. Our uneasy hiatus ended as the Squire clapped his hands.

"Fiddlers, where are you? Then fiddle and let us enjoy our Harvest Home."

I cannot say that the Harvest Home at Widdington Farm was as merry an evening that might have occurred for the presence of the Squire surely inhibited the pleasures of a rare and hearty meal for the harvesters. I gazed upon the rows of stiffly assembled rustics within the old barn that was bedecked with greenery and observed the crooked backs, stooped necks and the course hands that spoke of years of faithful toil in the fields about Uphaven. The very old were not forgotten and sat welcomed amongst the throng, their labours now spent but I witnessed the spectre of hunger upon these country faces, young and old together. It requires only a poor harvest for which the farmer will be set back but it is the labourer who shall survive upon the scraps of harvest. He also depends greatly upon the scraps of land that are now become enclosed by the quickset hedge as the progressive farmer seeks to embrace this efficiency as directed by the Board of Agriculture for I have before read Mr Arthur Young's recommendations upon my visits to the British Museum library. I gave my plum pudding to a young brother and sister and stole away to the shadows to sleep amongst the remaining stooks upon the harvest wagon and left Widdington Farm after the cockerel burst asunder my dreams.

I encountered a dead horse upon the road in Figheldean with no person in sight and I could only surmise that arrangements were being made for its collection. To view a lifeless thing it is a miraculous puzzle as to how life itself can animate a collection of muscle, bone, tendon, sinew, and organs. Beyond the village of Durrington I beat a path with my thumbstick to enable me to bathe in the river Avon for I was hot from the labour of carrying my weighty pack but also to remove the itching dust from my night in the corn wagon. The water had an earthy smell and was not overly deep but as I cannot swim I was happy to spread my arms wide to float a while, tilting my head back to stare up at the drifting clouds. Amidst these conflicting but gentle motions it was as if my mind was being drawn in opposing directions and with no solid ground to affix me I was instead suspended somewhere betwixt earth and sky. In time I was forced to walk upon the stony bed against the push of the river with a tangle of snaking weed about my legs to return upstream. Between the stinging nettle and the bramble there was no place to rest in comfort and so I chose instead the short grass in the field above the river bank to lay down and dry my skin in the sun. I may have lain naked for longer if it were not for a persistent and silent long grey fly that attacked my skin leaving raised lumps. There is a vast circular earthwork not one hundred paces from the river that sits upon ground tilted heavily to the east and indeed the entrance is at the lowest point on this eastern side. It is, I believe, called Durrington Walls and has a vast bank and inner ditch, much in the manner of the work at Marden where is enclosed the enormous man made hill. There is no hill at Durrington but it is indeed a work of great magnitude and so close in distance to Stonehenge that I cannot believe that the two places did not have some ancient association. Upon the way to my destination I encountered a lone sarcen stone recumbent in a field that does not readily explain itself other than perhaps it is a marker or indeed a runty straggler that did not complete its journey to the stone circle. The Cursus is then met which is itself a huge ancient undertaking comprising of two parallel banks with a broad expanse of level ground between these boundaries. The work is ruler straight and exceeds a mile in length and was first identified by that keen seeker out of antiquities, Mr William Stukeley who thought it an ancient course for a chariot race and it has therefore become the "Cursus" whether it be intended for that purpose or not. There are many features that are given names but they only serve as a convenient nomenclature for their origins and titles are lost to us. Stonehenge is another such name, for we must call it something. Ahead I could now see the object of my excursion and I walked there directly from the eastern conclusion of the Cursus. There is a small valley between these two places where all sight of Stonehenge is lost but it rises again with powerful intent upon the horizon for I had now joined the alignment of the ancient processional Avenue. On this occasion the shepherds were elsewhere and I shuddered as I entered the building, for it is indeed a great building my dear uncle. I rested upon the green sward with my back to one of the larger upright sarcen stones and there I began to weep. After fulfilling the walk that my father once proposed I had no further expectation of bridging the void between life and death, but through a blur of tears I then witnessed a flickering of bright colour and there briefly upon the grass before me alighted a butterfly with its wings spread wide to savour the warming afternoon sun. I rubbed at my eyes to ensure that it was not a trick of the mind but here with the same crisp scarlet and white markings imprinted upon black velvet was the butterfly that had prompted my early departure from Southwark. No sooner had it appeared then it fluttered away across Stonehenge Down and as the sheep began to drift back amongst the great standing stones I left this sacred place with my heart soaring for in that brief moment all was as it should be and heaven and earth were in accord.

*

As tired as I am my dear uncle and with my bed beckoning I must hastily document an incident that occurred this evening. Upon joining Mr John Fenton for a late dinner and despite there only being the two of us in our small parlour, an occasion was called for. At the conclusion of our meal John announced that regardless of our lowly number, we were required to perform our antiquarian duty to determine the will of the god's with regard to our success at the opening of the barrows upon Stonehenge Down in the morning. Our table was cleared of all but our goblets that were filled to brim with wine and Mr Morgan, the landlord, was sought with a request for a silver bowl that was placed between us. From his pocket John produced four small tablets of bone and I now understood the purpose of this preparation for I had heard mention before of the Conjuror's Playthings. Not two years ago, under the guidance of Mr Cunnington with the two Mr Parker's, a number of barrows were opened upon Wilsford Down by the landowner Mr Edward Duke of Lake. Amongst a plethora of the more expected treasures retrieved during this short but prolific campaign were four unusual small engraved bone tablets of which replicas were made at the request of Mr Cunnington. These facsimiles were dubbed "The Conjuror's Playthings" by Mr Cunnington who presented the set to Sir Richard Colt Hoare with a written description of the likely outcome at the casting of these lots. They were now inexplicably in the hands of Mr John Fenton who claimed to be looking after them for his father. I requested to inspect these mysterious objects where the

The conjuror's Playthings

original engraved design had now been replicated in red ink. Upon each face of the tablets a different pattern was depicted apart from one tablet that was blank on both sides.

John was impatient to get started whilst I wished to discuss the significance of such a discovery for surely this was as close to an ornament of ancient writing that had yet been brought to the attention of the antiquary.

"Yes, yes Henry, place them in the silver bowl and we must now stand and turn to the east..with our goblets in hand."

Whilst standing I read from the list of various permutations that had been contrived by Mr Cunnington for the purpose of antiquarian entertainment before embarking upon further barrow excavation. I shall not record them all for you my dear uncle but a poor return may state; "You will not attain your ends. Stay at home." whilst a more encouraging indication of success might read: "Full completion of your wishes". Once the bowl has been upturned it shall be the tablet that settles farthest from the bowl that determines the outcome of this mystical consultation.

After drinking deeply from his goblet, John vigorously cast the Conjuror's Playthings from the silver bowl whereupon one tablet tumbled from the table and despite our hasty examination of the floor we could find no trace of it. At that moment the parlour door was nosed open by the yard dog and being quicker in thought and action, the animal spied the tablet of bone upon the flagstones and hastily gobbled it up. The dog was then kicked back out into the yard by the landlord with the parlour door slammed shut.

John slumped back into his chair and attempted to feign unconcern at the loss of the tablet but was soon at the door peering out into the dusk, hissing and making faces at the dog as it skulked in the yard. I then excused myself for I had yet to conclude my account of last evening and indeed of my journey today. Before departing I suggested to John that it did not require a list of possible outcomes to know that a dog eating the prophetic tablet was not at all a good omen. John Fenton growled in response before refilling his goblet and continued his vigil at the open door;

"Accursed animal, Henry is there a chance that the piece shall reappear…..in the morning..or perhaps I may be able to induce the thing to wretch?"

I wish you a good night my dear uncle and I hold no doubt that I shall sleep soundly in my bed.

Your weary Nephew,
HENRY CHALK

POSTSCRIPT

There are two more issues that I must record to clear my mind and to enable a blank canvas upon which to dream. My flint sickle is lost, despite my polite request for its return. I dared not mention it to the Squire and so it is left behind at Widdington Farm. May their future harvests be blessed and bountiful and perhaps the ancient flint sickle shall again perform the final act of harvest. In due course I will conclude a drawing that I began when the piece was in my possession so that you may obtain some idea of its form.

I realise also that I have not given an account of my repaired boot for I at first cursed the tardy cobbler in Beckhampton and I am now ashamed at my earlier impatience for the cobbler had been taken gravely ill and indeed it was his young daughter that completed the repair of my boot. Upon its return Boots disparaged the quality of the finished work for it was perhaps not the neatest stitching but I believe that it will hold well enough and I gave Boots a half crown for the cobbler's family in addition to the cost of the repair.

Monday 5th September 1808

MY DEAR UNCLE,

It has indeed been a most eventful day and I can report that antiquarians far and wide shall marvel at the work undertaken upon Stonehenge Down by Mr William Cunnington and his two stalwart labourers Mr Stephen and John Parker.

After a comfortable night I arose very late from my bed and upon the completion of a fine breakfast I read a portion of Gulliver's Travels but in time I made my excuses to a fretful Mr John Fenton for I could no longer resist the urges of my feet. I explained that I would meet with Mr William Cunnington and his party upon Stonehenge Down although I hoped not to offend by my restless nature. John stated that he must await their arrival at the George Inn, lest there be any confusion on the matter and he wondered at their lateness for the appointed hour had come and gone with no sign of our friends. I had been informed that the day's activity lay to the South of Stonehenge and so upon leaving the town of Amesbury and crossing the River Avon I sought a deviation from the toll road and was soon rewarded upon my ramble with a fine view across

Stonehenge Down. It is no surprise to find a plump barrow at this location for it commands perhaps the highest aspect of the many tumuli that gather about Stonehenge. The stone circle stands dwarfed by its surrounds not a mile distant from this vantage point and is surely the hub of a vast and ancient graveyard. The tombs of these lost dynasties cluster together in mysterious affiliation upon the crests and elevations where Stonehenge must remain in view and to good advantage. A distant glimpse of whiteness, as the sun flared between passing cloud, signalled the position across the valley of the morning's toil by Mr Cunnington's two barrow diggers for the freshly exposed chalk shone like a beacon amidst the dry green hues of late summer. With this fortuitous guidance I left my lofty tree covered barrow and hurried to the conspicuous tumuli in expectation of witnessing the revealed secrets of the ancients. I found instead the two labourers laying in stillness, side by side, upon the summit of the barrow with the gaping excavation at their feet as if they themselves were awaiting burial. The gentle purring of contented sleep betrayed the notion of eternal rest for after the consumption of their victuals, Mr Stephen and John Parker, the two most experienced barrow diggers in the land, were now engaged in peaceful slumber. In my attempt at a stealthy retreat I tipped a nodule of chalk into the deep hollow with my boot, waking Mr John Parker with a start and he was soon to his feet in animated confusion, turning full circle upon the barrow for sight of Mr Cunnington and his party. Spying no one but myself he slowly retrieved his hat from the grass and employed it to give his father a gentle nudge.

"Bist git aan vather."

With reluctance Mr Stephen Parker relinquished the opium of pleasurable sleep and coughed himself awake before being hauled unsteadily to his feet by his son. I now felt at fault at this interruption to their rest and we stood in silence as the sun broke free into open sky to glare upon the chalk that surrounded us. I offered my name and explained that we had met before upon two separate occasions and the two men nodded together in sullen acknowledgement of this fact, touching their hats as they did so.

"Mizzer Chalk zur."

The elder of the two labourers bent stiffly to gather his tools, adding his beer to the bucket and with a pick axe over his shoulder he plodded slowly away between the neighbouring tumuli. I felt bound to ask John Parker, as he collected his own tools as to the prospects of the present excavation that lay open before us.

In response he retrieved some large shards of ancient pottery from a heap of spoil and held them out for my inspection pointing to where they had been struck previously by a pick axe.

"T'wur avore we. Robbers zee, zo dwon't spec much wur no zense."

I have learned subsequently that the two labourers were

surely deserving of their rest after leaving Heytesbury on
foot in the early morning with their tools to commence
opening barrows upon Stonehenge Down before I had
stirred from my bed.

Stephen and John Parker now turned their attentions
to the famous "Bush Barrow", so named for it displayed
a crown of furze upon its summit and it was evident that
a large portion of the tomb was already open and exposed
to the elements. Father and son were still muttering to
one another as to where they should begin their renewed
examination within the open barrow when Mr Cunnington's
carriage finally arrived and the quietude of Stonehenge
Down was replaced by the fluster and hub-bub of greetings
and introductions.

It was a pleasure to meet again with Mr William
Cunnington who greeted me warmly as did Mr Philip
Crocker. I was then introduced to Mrs Mary Cunnington
and their youngest daughter Ann, whom I judge to be near
to my own age. There followed a collective enquiry into
my wellbeing after my near burial upon the plain behind
the Winterslow Hut. I reddened as a consequence of this
attention and Miss Ann Cunnington now suggested that I
should be considered a fully fledged antiquarian after such
heroic deeds. I answered that if it were also a requirement
to be a fool then I assuredly did qualify in that regard.

"Fools are we all in the eyes of our detractors.." stated
Mr Cunnington "..and it is certainly a fool who neglects his

own business to disturb the dust of our ancestors."

"Papa.." retorted his daughter sharply "You are never a fool and you must not say so."

I remained silent upon the subject of my own business that appeared to prosper well enough without my interference.

I was keen to enquire after Mr Cunnington's health for I am aware of the frequent and debilitating headaches from which he suffers. Mrs Mary Cunnington answered my concern by stating that their late arrival today was as a consequence of a poor night for Mr Cunnington.

"We are here out of fortitude Mr Chalk and it is no secret that I regard the demands placed upon my husband to be contributory to the frequency of these attacks."

Mr Cunnington took his wife's hand and tutted softly that she must not exaggerate this claim.

"I have yet to encounter a barrow or any place of interest to the antiquary where fresh air does not exist in plentiful supply and is indeed the best prescription for my condition."

He paused to take a deep breath as if to emphasize this statement.

"There..it is a fine day for opening barrows. Indeed if we should have cast the Conjuror's Playthings, as is our custom Henry, then perhaps the God's may have granted us the full completion of our wishes."

Mr John Fenton having just emerged yawning from the

carriage coughed suddenly in alarm at the mention of the
Conjuror's Playthings and was quick to blame an intrusive
fly for this outburst. He was equally keen to steer the
subject away to new territories and suggested that he may
soon play upon his flute, once he had wet his lips and also
flushed the uninvited fly from his gullet and that a glass of
wine was probably the best solution to achieve both these
ends.

"John, you are become more like your father each time
we meet" laughed Mr Philip Crocker.

Whilst our belated lunch was being prepared Mr
Cunnington consulted with the two Mr Parker's as to the
outcome of their morning's labour and also how the renewed
examination of Bush Barrow should now be conducted.
Upon his return we made ourselves comfortable upon a
patchwork of blankets beside the barrow and enjoyed a
convivial lunch accompanied by the intermittent clomp of
the pick axe and the slow scrape of the shovel. For my
benefit our host described the frustration of the previous
attempt upon this same barrow in July of this year.

"Henry, never before have I known a greater condition
of expectation as existed upon that day for Mr William
Stukeley in his great book of Stonehenge has drawn the
attention of every antiquary to the singular presence of
Bush Barrow."

Ann Cunnington then eagerly supplied the names of
the esteemed company who had gathered together in such

anticipation.

"The Reverend Iremonger from Wherwell and the Reverend Weston. Mr and Mrs Lambert from Boyton. Mr and Mrs Rackett and also the geologist Mr Sowerby."

Her father then lowered his voice to continue.

"John Parker in particular was greatly vexed at this failure before the eyes of our learned friends. Indeed today he and his father are in a decidedly grumpy condition and I am at a loss to understand the cause lest it should be the memory of that day."

John Fenton stated loudly that it was now his duty to inspire our barrow diggers and also to appease the disturbed spirits of Bush Barrow by climbing the mound to play upon his flute. This musical offering soon prompted great billows of tobacco smoke to rise from within the tomb as if it were now of a sudden a smouldering volcano contemplating eruption. Having successfully accelerated the pace of the clomp and the scrape, John lay down his flute and Mr Philip Crocker enquired as to the details of my pedestrian excursion;

"Henry, I understand that you arrived upon foot from Marlborough and not as we expected directly from London?"

Sir, you see that I am still to be mollycoddled.

I related the episodes of my excursion, lamenting that I could not show the fine flint piece that I retrieved from the sandy soils that exist to the North of Salisbury Plain.

I then queried as to whether an antiquarian investigation had taken place into the huge mound situated in the village of Marden whereupon I was informed that a full ten days of labour had been undertaken there last year by Mr Cunnington accompanied by the two Mr Parker's and a team of local men. Nothing but a few burnt bones, ashes and a slither of wood were retrieved after such Herculean labour into these unstable sandy soils but Mr Cunnington proposed that its purpose was indeed sepulchral.

"Others would have it as a Hill Altar but I maintain that we did not find the primary interment, Henry you have seen for yourself the size of the undertaking and it was akin to searching for a needle in a haystack. We could spend no more upon the great Hatfield Barrow and so I called the men from their work."

Mr Crocker stated in a serious tone that disaster was narrowly averted for without warning the great cutting within the barrow slumped down into the enormous excavation only moments after Mr Cunnington had called a judicious halt to proceedings.

"Indeed Mr John Parker was reluctant to cease the work and would be down there still I fear. Sand does not behave like chalk Henry."

John Fenton reminded our gathering that I still managed to become buried under chalk nevertheless but agreed that good fortune and common sense had certainly prevailed at Marden.

I was then urged to continue with the account of my journey whilst there was a deal of questions I still wished to ask about Marden and its surrounds for Mr Cunnington strongly asserted that these ancient works were second only to Avebury and Stonehenge in their importance.

"Henry we shall visit together, on a good day."

I progressed to my meeting with the Reverend Joseph Townsend and now fully intended to reveal how the Vicar of Pewsey held the most unchristian sympathies toward the plight of the labouring poor. Indeed, I had not the opportunity to continue for Mr William Cunnington's face lit up at the mention of this gentleman's name for he clearly held the Reverend Joseph Townsend in the highest regard.

"He possesses an extraordinary collection of fossils and has found new examples amongst the greensands about the village of Pewsey. Indeed Henry you no doubt discussed the origins of flint for it is a subject that is close to both your hearts. My good friend has informed me recently that the creation of this mysterious substance is due entirely to the decomposition of different marine bodies for it is these fossil remnants that universally form the nucleus of flint. This was a most fortuitous encounter Henry."

Mr Philip Crocker supported this view and spoke of his admiration for the Reverend Joseph Townsend of Pewsey.

"He surely informed you that he is the commissioner for all turnpike roads within the county of Wiltshire, though he may be unaware that he is referred to fondly as "The

Colossus of Roads"."

Mr Cunnington continued the litany of achievements of this same gentleman;

"He has travelled widely and his publication "A Journey through Spain" is most enlightening in many regards. Did he not also invent a machine for the grinding of cocoa beans? I believe he did."

In turn Mrs Mary Cunnington confirmed her own appreciation for the broad talents of the vicar of Pewsey.

"He is a fine doctor to his flock and has published the most indispensible medical volume entitled the "The Physicians Vade Mecum" and I refer to it regularly and indeed no good home should be without it."

"I must correspond at the earliest opportunity Henry…" Confirmed her husband "..and I shall certainly send your regards to my good friend. It is well met, very well met indeed."

I hastily assured Mr Cunnington that it was a brief meeting and of little consequence for this gentleman would surely not recall a passing traveller when he has so much else to consider. Wishing to avoid all further reference to the Reverend Joseph Townsend I hurriedly moved on to explain that I had met another gentleman on my journey who proclaimed himself to be a champion of the poor and indeed held aspirations to become a member of Parliament himself. I stated that if he were to succeed then surely he would gain the support of any decent freeholder for the struggles of the labouring poor were plain for all to see.

"Indeed Henry.." observed John Fenton "..then you have been busy socialising when I thought that you were engaged in pedestrianism".

Miss Ann Cunnington enquired as to the name of this gentleman and upon announcing him to be Mr Henry Hunt I may instead have stated that I was associating with the d*v*l himself such was the reaction of our party.

"That despicable man!" exhorted Mrs Mary Cunnington.

Miss Ann Cunnington shot her eyes wide in alarm and clapped her hands to her mouth to stifle a scream whilst Mr William Cunnington frowned deeply as glances were exchanged. He then addressed me kindly;

"Mr Hunt is not a person with whom you should associate Henry for he is a ..a..a...I cannot say what he is.. and.. we shall not speak of him again."

Thus the account of my journey ended abruptly as bulky white clouds cast great creeping shadows across Stonehenge Down and I was left to reflect that I am perhaps a poor judge of character. In the ensuing silence I withdrew to make a drawing to encompass the scene, whilst Ann Cunnington positioned herself at my shoulder in order to observe my humble efforts. As I sat with pencil in hand Ann then took pleasure in whispering the deeds of Mr Henry Hunt who it seems tore his own marriage asunder and took another man's wife for a mistress.

"Mama would not like to think that I know of such

matters but everyone knows how Mr Henry Hunt became persona non grata. No gentleman will entertain him though he holds a passion for sports of the field but his hunters stand idle in the stable and he may shoot no pheasant but his own. He has three children and the two boys are raised at the home of the mistress. He is handsome and Papa says he is a Jacobin and a very dangerous man."

To temper the obvious pleasure in relating such scandal I maintained a steady line with my pencil and a prudent silence but I cannot pretend that such close attention shall ever assist the artist however modest their aspirations.

We rejoined the party and I took my turn to climb the mound and observe the steaming backs of the two Mr Parker's for there appeared no end to the amounts of chalky soil to be moved from here to there. Miss Ann Cunnington had just proposed a game entitled "A Fool's Bolt" where we were obliged to provide a fanciful theory as to the origins of Stonehenge when Mr Crocker cocked an ear and indeed the steady clomp of the pick and slow scrape of the shovel had now ceased. As we listened to the silence upon Stonehenge Down there followed a single word of encouragement called out from within the tomb.

"Zurr."

Upon this one rustic syllable the expectations of our own party were now drawn and we hastened to gather at the rim of the excavation to find the two labourers kneeling upon the earth at a depth of eight feet or more in the very heart of the barrow. A number of ledges had been formed upon which the work had been staged and with Mr Cunnington and Mr Philip Crocker I was encouraged to descend as far as we were able until we stood pressed together upon a narrow ledge of chalky soil. A circle of soil stained bone had been revealed which indeed proved to be the skull of the occupant of Bush Barrow and the two Mr Parker's now cast aside their crude tools to adopt instead a pair of small trowels. I learnt that the patron for these antiquarian excursions Sir Richard Colt Hoare had presented father and son with these "barrow knives" especially manufactured for the task of delicate excavation and they were considered as badges of honour by the two men.

A discourse between John Parker and Mr Cunnington confirmed that the burial was placed upon the original surface of Stonehenge Down and not as expected within a grave or cist. John Parker now began to scrape at the soil around the skull and it was soon evident that the body had been lain with the head to the south. In an area between the skull and our own close position, a number of rivets were picked from the soil with also the fine remains of decayed wood and thin crumbling strips of brass. For the benefit of our party Mr Cunnington conveyed the information that an object had been placed above the head at the burial but had not survived. John Parker then shuffled along within the cramped hollow between the wall of chalk and the still submerged occupant of the tomb and now displayed a wide eyed keenness for the task that lay before him. The deep shadow at this depth made it sorely difficult to view with any clarity and whilst John Parker worked with his nose to the soil his father sat back and lit a pipe to fill the hollow with tobacco smoke prompting Mrs Mary Cunnington to cough and soon protest at this action;

"Mr Stephen there is little enough air to breath without the botheration of your pipe."

"Zurry Maam."

The sound of metal striking upon metal made us lean forward and as the soil was pared away from this new object we could see it to be the head of an elegant axe with a broad splayed cutting edge. With care the axe was lifted upon the trowel and if any wood remained clad about the top of the piece it quickly crumbled away with the soil. The axe was passed to Mr Cunnington who held it flat upon his palm for us to view.

"The orientation of the body itself is most uncommon and neither is it contained within a cist as we might expect and now we find an axe."

The piece was passed to Mr Fenton and it was in turn conveyed to Ann Cunnington who in preparation had a square sheet of canvas laid out upon the summit of the barrow to receive each newly retrieved object.

John Parker was now making short work of burying my boots beneath a mass of soil flicked from his trowel when a bright green object was revealed that appeared to glow in the shadowy light. The blade of a dagger had suffered from its exposure to the soil and this corrosion was termed "virdigris" by Mr Cunnington. A further piece believed to be the handle or its remains was also passed with care to the summit of the barrow. No sooner had one luminous green blade been extracted from beside the skeleton's torso than a longer piece was discovered which was deemed to be a lance for it was laid pointing upwards as if once attached to a shaft. John Parker now crouched low above the trowel and with the deftest touch revealed a small object that confirmed itself to be gold once the soil had been smudged away under his thumb. It is the nature of gold to remain unchanged in the soil and through our fingers passed an ornamented object that once adorned the occupant of Bush Barrow as a buckle or hasp for there was a hook upon one face of the piece. Mr Philip Crocker stated quietly that gold is rarely found in isolation in such circumstances and amongst this southerly cluster of barrows on Stonehenge Down gold objects have already been retrieved which only served to fuel our sense of anticipation. John Parker continued with the steady removal of the soil beneath the delicate bones of the right hand where a further lance of brass was discovered but did not survive its extrication from the soil.

"Tes awl bruckley zur.." lamented the younger excavator looking up to Mr Cunnington as the piece dissolved before our eyes, the metal being so rotten that all structure was lost. John Parker sighed deeply and moved the point of his trowel to the collapsed ribs of the skeleton and the frustration of the decayed lance was soon forgot for there centrally placed upon the chest was an object that made our eyes widen in disbelief and we regarded one another in silent wonder. A large engraved gold breast plate in lozenge form that Mr Crocker later measured as six by seven inches had evidently been worn by the deceased at burial. The thin gold sheet was once attached to a wooden backing which had not survived the years nor the remaining fragments from its extraction from the soil.

Mr William Cunnington pronounced that we should think now of our generous patron Sir Richard Colt Hoare for how he would have relished the conquest of Bush Barrow had he not been conducting a further tour of Wales with Mr Richard Fenton.

With the gold lozenge now glistening in the sun upon the summit of the barrow our attention was drawn again to what lay yet to be discovered and Mr Stephen Parker now continued down the right hand side of the skeleton from the skull and around the jumble of bones that once formed the backbone. Not a word was spoken and in due course the elder excavator was rewarded for his patience in revealing a stone mace head perforated by a central hole with a small metal ring that perhaps assisted with securing the piece to a wooden shaft. To accompany the polished stone a number of puzzling rings of bone were recovered that may have adorned a long vanished handle. With a hint of satisfaction Mr Stephen Parker straightened his back and held up a smaller engraved gold lozenge which proved to be the final success of the day, save for a jumble of beads retrieved from the soil.

As the excavators continued to reveal the remainder of the skeleton, Mr Philip Crocker measured the thigh bone and found it to be twenty and a half inches in length whereupon Stephen Parker proclaimed their subject to be "A gurt lanky zart o' a man".

Leaving the two men to complete their work we clambered shivering from the tomb to be enveloped by a warm and golden light with our shadows cast long across the plain. I paused at the summit to look down once more upon the scene below, at the crouched and soil tarnished fossil of a man and the two labourers charged with revealing his long buried secrets. Sir, I confess to be envious of their task for I have experienced once before upon the plains behind the Winterslow Hut, the pains and successes of such physical labour when the body is engaged but the mind shall rove freely. Mr John Parker has I believe an education born from his experience and the considerations of both Mr Parkers are sought by Mr Cunnington for he values greatly their ability and judgement in what I shall term a practical antiquarianism. I wished to engage with these taciturn countrymen but suspected that despite the

The Excavation of Bush Barrow

fine success of the day I had not yet been forgiven for disturbing their noontime slumber. The two excavators slowly emerged from Bush Barrow and as with all our party they appeared to relish the late afternoon sun after their time spent in the cold shadow of the tomb. I was soon to be left alone upon the summit and noted how this broad mound occupies a position of crowning glory on this swell of barrow populated down land to the South of Stonehenge. I then drew the attention of our departing party to some activity near the stone circle itself and what appeared to be the raising of small tents but none could offer an explanation until an approaching farmer upon horseback soon accounted for this mystery whilst we gathered about our carriage.

"Tus fer a game o'cricket on the morrow, yus."

The farmer then asked after our own activity and Miss Ann Cunnington displayed proudly the freshly revealed secrets of Bush Barrow to which he responded by scratching his head under an old felt hat.

"Wull, I know'd green burrow awl me loife but nuver did zee zich a thing avore."

Being a practical man he pointed to the stone mace and pronounced it as the handle for a gimlet, making a screwing action with his wrist.

"Ah vur a gimlet if you asks me ladies and gent'mun."

At this we all departed for Amesbury with Stephen and John Parker travelling beside the driver leaving the occupant of Bush Barrow exposed to the dry air of these chalklands for the visit of Sir Richard Colt Hoare upon his return to Wiltshire.

Due libations were made at dinner and the buffed gold was presented at the table drawing much attention from a growing throng of cricketers and their supporters at the George Inn, with whom Mr John Fenton is now carousing happily. I have not imbibed greatly but slipped away to write my account of this truly astonishing day and prey forgive my indulgence in that regard.

I still crave correspondence from you my dear uncle and a single word or two would be sufficient to calm my great concern for your own well being for it is a silence that dwells so heavily upon me with each passing day.

Your expectant Nephew
HENRY CHALK

*

POSTSCRIPT.
Upon the removal of my boots I have found inside a quantity of fine soil and was able to pour out a small pile from each boot into my hand. I can only surmise that this occurred when Mr John Parker heaped the soil from his trowel about my feet and indeed the soil entered freely through the tops of my boots. Had I not noticed a curious glinting amongst this soil before the candle then I would have cast it out into the night from the window and so instead, in my stockinged feet, I sought out Mr Philip Crocker to borrow

a glass to make a closer inspection. Mr Crocker explained that Mr Cunnington had the glass and we together knocked quietly upon his door and as they were not yet abed we were invited in. To keep the soil from dispersing I had tipped it into my fob pocket and I now extracted a pinch to study under the glass and we found there to be a multitude of minute gold pins amongst the soil. I recounted the occasion of the burying of my boots by John Parker and that it had occurred at the recovery of the dagger and lance. Mr Crocker soon returned with the dagger and also the soil encrusted handle and a careful examination revealed that a portion of the wood from the handle remained intact and displayed a fine zig-zag design constructed entirely from a tight arrangement of these same gold pins. We all looked at one another for we could not comprehend the scale of this undertaking for no glass would have existed in ancient times and the pins were surely too small for the keenest eye or indeed the nimblest fingers.

Our host then summed up our thoughts at this discovery;

"We wonder at the most conspicuous achievements of our ancient ancestors with the creation of stone circles and the raising of great mounds and yet here is an undertaking of an opposing scale that is surely no less astonishing. Tomorrow we shall return and ensure that John recovers from the soil more of these extraordinary gold pins. Today the God's have indeed granted the full completion of our wishes to exceed perhaps even our greatest expectations, goodnight gentlemen."

I shall now read awhile from Gulliver's Travels for Mr Swift's tale is no stranger to such extremes in scale and perhaps it was after all a resident of Lilliput that was engaged to decorate the handle of the dagger.

Tuesday 6th September 1808

MY DEAR UNCLE,

After the events of yesterday you may believe Sir that my well of excitement is near exhausted but there is to be a game of cricket held upon Stonehenge Down and whilst at breakfast I have been informed that I am to participate. The game is to extend for two whole days and Mr William Cunnington has graciously excused both John and myself from our antiquarian duties, such as they are, with the blessing that as young men we must enjoy ourselves whilst we can. Miss Ann Cunnington has stated that it is a fine distraction from the important business of becoming better acquainted with our ancient ancestors but she now wishes us success in our "frivolous pursuit".

I understand that two members of the cricket team cannot now attend the game and as John Fenton had spent a long evening extolling his virtues as a cricketer we are now to join the home team. John has informed me that if any person should ask then I am to say that I am a cricketer also. When I enquire of John what shall be expected of us he only shrugs his shoulders and complains of a heavy head and in the cold light of day he now confesses quietly to me that he knows nothing of the game.

There have been many new arrivals at the George Inn who are filled with talk of the game of cricket and this only serves to excite me further. The gentlemen of the opposing team are mustering in the parlour although they await the "Players" who I understand to be the experienced and regular cricketers. Indeed there is some anxiety by our own side to establish the identity of these men and many likely names have been uttered. The Players in our home side are indeed not young men and I gauge by the mutterings of our own gentlemen, as the bowls of punch are circulated, that they are not known by reputation. I am now squeezed into the corner of the parlour and I shall report later, my dear uncle, on the events of the day.

Before I conclude there are now gasps of surprise, and indeed dismay, from our team with the news that Silver Billy has just this minute arrived at the George Inn. The opposing captain is as smug as a cat that has lapped the cream but as I know nothing of cricket or the men who play it I can only surmise that Mr William Beldham, or Silver Billy as he is also known, is a fine player indeed.

*

Sir, I am just returned from Stonehenge Down and I have now hastily concealed myself in my room. There is much gloom and confusion amongst the participants of both teams for the outcome of the day has been most unsatisfactory and to some degree I am indeed culpable.

As the Gentlemen and Players grumble and disperse from the George Inn, it will serve you best my dear uncle if I describe the events of the day in the order that they occurred. For once Stonehenge itself was not the object of our attention and it served only as the dramatic scenery for our most curious activity. Four tents had been erected in advance of our arrival with bunting and flags strung between them and indeed this festooned tentage gave the appearance of a small pageant. The day was set fair but with a gusty breeze that worked the flags and sent great white clouds scudding before a blue sky.

Cricket is neither a race nor a straight fight but it is more a chivalrous battle where the batsman is required to defend his battlements from the small hurtling red leather cannonball. The two "armies" have professional soldiers within their ranks who are well versed in all the elements of this warfare and they are termed the "Players". The gentlemen who comprise the remainder of the team, with the exception of the rustic "long stop", are surely superior in the natural state of affairs but in this egalitarian pursuit the advantage must be held by the best cricketers. The gentlemen, however, must be at the top of the order when it comes to batting and such a list was posted before the commencement of the game. Indeed I considered it a miracle that overnight I had of a sudden become a cricketer and felt emboldened by the sight of my name upon this list although I had never touched a bat or a ball in my life. John Fenton was placed at nine and I was to follow at number ten whilst the "players" in our team were positioned at seven and eight. John Fenton then stated that our lowly placements were due to our being late additions to the team and he then grumbled that we were only "making up the numbers".

Both teams must provide an "umpire" to stand upon the field of play beside the wickets and these men are the upholders of the laws of cricket once the game is set. The umpires have cocked hats and are also required to carry a bat and it is but another inexplicable facet of this game for they only lean upon these bats and they are not required to strike the ball for any reason. Finally Sir, the score is kept by two men who sit in the outfield upon a bench and they record each run made with a notch cut into a tally stick. Indeed it is the simplest aspect of this game of cricket for the team with the most notches at the end of the proceedings wins the game. The prize for the winning team is eleven guineas and eleven pairs of gloves but I understand that a great deal more than eleven guineas may be wagered with the bookmakers who are also present here on Stonehenge Down.

With the toss of a coin between the two captains, it was thereby determined that the home team should bat first and our gentlemen prepared themselves in the privacy of our tent. The opposing team then strode out onto the Stonehenge turf, smartly attired in colourful matching caps and received great applause from their supporters. Soon after, the two home batsmen appeared and they too were heartily clapped and encouraged by the burgeoning crowd. There was indeed now a wonderful sense of occasion and expectancy upon Stonehenge Down with this gathering of cricketers and their supporters and my heart raced with the thought that I would also be participating in this thrilling contest. Our "innings" however did not begin well for there are many ways for a batter to fail in his task and be judged "out" by the umpire and the gentlemen in our team soon explored all possibilities in this regard whilst the supporters of both teams cheered and groaned respectively with the fall of each wicket. Our two "Players" spent a deal more time at the wicket demonstrating stout defence but did not add many notches to the tally-stick before they to were dismissed by the scuttling ball. John Fenton was summoned in a rush from the victual tent and had no sooner arrived at the wicket when he was "run out" without the bother of having to face the bowler at all. On his return he dropped the cricket bat at my feet and offered a word of caution before going in search of his glass of wine that had been hastily abandoned only moments before;

"Pray beware Henry for our man will not move one inch when there is a good run to be taken."

It is indeed a long walk to the wicket with the eyes of the opposing team upon you. One of the "Players" in our side had shown me how to stuff padding into the front of my stockings to protect my shins from the hard ball and I at first felt foolish with these lumpy additions protruding before me. My jovial partner greeted me at the wicket and appeared wholly unconcerned by our lack of notches thus far and then proceeded to list the viands that he would heap upon his plate once lunch was taken.

The bowlers begin their run with the ball held aloft and stride in with gathering speed to hurl the ball as might a man playing at skittles but with a greater elevation to enable the ball to land before the batsman. The scuttling ball must be kept out at all costs but my first delivery bounced away to the side and I spun around in a full circle as I followed its course but bat and ball made no contact. Some distance behind the wicket keeper is where the "long stop" stands and he is neither a gentleman nor a player but instead a rustic who is expected to dirty his knees in stopping the ball. From this distant position I could hear this countryman's voice calling out after my first failed attempt;

"Look at 'is 'ead up in the air loike a goose."

As the bowler paced back to his mark I pictured a honking goose in my mind and decided that I would instead keep my head low whereupon the long necked goose was swiftly replaced by a snuffling pig. I now afford myself some mild amusement at these farmyard analogies but with my head down I was at least able to observe the ball as it hit the bat. At the forth ball bowled I played it firmly

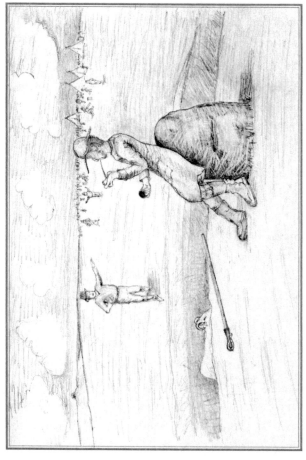

The Cricket Match at Stonehenge

away and a run was taken with plenty of time for my jovial partner to make his ground once I had arrived beside him and politely urged him to leave his position. I now faced the bowling of Silver Billy who had already accounted for a great number of our team. Indeed I heard it whispered by their captain that this was to be Silver Billy's final "over" before he was to be replaced by a new bowler and so I defended my wicket for all I was worth. With the forth and final ball I then surprised myself by striking a pleasant shot straight back beyond Silver Billy and I pressed my fellow batter to run three and near caught him up upon taking the third run.

"Mr Chalk... Mr Chalk" he puffed, "Such exertion before lunch.. is unwise..."

At the next opportunity my red faced partner flatly refused to leave his crease despite there being plenty of time to make a run.

"Young Sir, you have again kept me from feasting upon the ball and it is unfair. It is now my turn."

This gentleman was oblivious to the slender margins of his survival as the whistling ball shaved the wickets or bounced directly over the bail. With the bowler thundering in beside me I could but close my eyes and pray whilst the opposing side would groan in unison as my partner again swished at thin air, drawing cries of desperation from the field.

"A straight ball PLEASE bowler."

For the sake of our team, when I next faced the bowling, I decided to smite the ball as far as I could and on three occasions it sped amongst the legs of the spectators and the cheering crowd parted to let the fielder to the ball whilst I urged my companion to keep running.

Finally my jovial partner struck a ball high up into the air and stood craning his neck to admire this splendid effort until he gauged with some panic that it was about to descend from whence it came and land directly upon his head. With a great cry of anxiety he leapt to the side to avoid this circumstance and as he lay sprawled upon the turf the ball was in turn caught by the wicket keeper and my companion was called out.

Our rustic long-stop was last man in and he trailed to the crease with the most doleful countenance as if he knew in advance the fate that was about to befall him. His first delivery then conspired to leap more than any previous ball of the morning and so struck the unfortunate man upon the head with a loud "tock" whereupon he collapsed back onto the three wickets to splay them in all directions. I helped long-stop Davis back to his feet with his brow now displaying a lump the size of a small egg and he staggered from the field muttering and shaking his head;

"I knew 'twud 'appen."

With our first innings now concluded the scorers announced that we had managed forty one notches of which my contribution was twenty eight. I felt a pat on

the back and turned to find that it was Silver Billy who
then shook my hand and studied me for a moment before
stating quietly that if it had not been for my efforts then
our score should be a paltry one indeed. A number of other
gentlemen repeated this gesture and the captain of the
opposing team declared loudly that;

"This young "goose" is far from cooked. Well done
young Mr Chalk."

Lunch was taken and in time we resumed the field of
play as belts were loosened and our captain ordered us to
spread ourselves about. The opposing gentleman batters
fared no better than our own men and notches upon the
tally stick were scarce. The Stonehenge turf accounted
for a number of wickets until the arrival of Silver Billy at
the crease. It appears that Silver Billy is indeed the most
heralded batsman in the land and our opposing captain
had paid dearly to secure his services such was the import
placed upon winning the game. My dear uncle to have
Mr William Beldham in your team is akin to securing the
services of the Late and beloved Admiral Nelson, may God
rest his soul, to participate in a gentleman's rowing match.
Of a sudden the game was no longer an even contest with
our fielders never occupying the correct positions to stop
the ball and our bowlers were very soon confounded.
Indeed wherever the ball pitched, Silver Billy was there to
pounce upon it with his feet moving like the most nimble
dancing master and with all the while a raised left elbow to

lead the stroke. The visiting supporters cheered each deft click as this master batsman struck the ball to all parts of Stonehenge Down and they then urged their man to run faster between the wickets;

"Tich and turn Billy, tich and turn."

The scorers notched upon the tally stick as fast as they were able with the pile of wood shavings mounting rapidly about their feet. Runs were taken with ease and our fielders retreated back to stand before the crowd but still we had not enough men on the field to prevent the ball from passing us by. I was fully prepared to fling myself at the ball to prevent its escape into the crowd as it sped across the turf and on two occasions I succeeded. At first I was unable to propel the ball back to the middle and indeed our two Players had quick arms in this regard but I was unable to emulate this method. I instead devised a means to lob the ball as if from an ancient battle machine called a trebuchet with my arm kept straight to whirl in a full circle alongside my ear and by this method some distance was gained.

Silver Billy had in turn punished all our regular bowlers so that none wished to meet the captain's eye and he scoured the field in desperation.

"You Sir."

I looked behind my position to see to whom this gesture was intended and soon realised, with no small degree of alarm, that I was now being summoned to bowl. My protestations were ignored and I found myself with ball in hand and with Silver Billy poised and ready to deal with my novice efforts. My first attempt sent the ball sailing high over the batsman's head and it was returned by long-stop Davis. The second ball was also greatly elevated but within reach of Silver Billy who slashed it high and far until it came to rest in the ditch that encircles Stonehenge. There was some muttering by our own side at the wisdom of this choice of bowler and with the pair of batsman panting at their running of ten runs, Mr John Fenton duly trotted up to me with ball in hand and placed an arm around my shoulder.

"Henry, we shall forever be chasing leather at this rate."

He lowered his voice and counselled me on how I should abandon the accepted method of bowling and instead emulate the means by which I was able to send the ball in from the outfield.

"Yes Henry "the trebuchet", you may call it what you will but I implore you to try it now."

As John Fenton returned to his position I settled at the end of my run before galloping towards the crouching silver haired batsman and with all my might I spun my arm over to release the ball. As a consequence of this great exertion I was sent sprawling upon the turf but was able to observe the trajectory of the ball as it speared in towards the master batsman's feet that had for once remained stationary at the crease such was his surprise at the nature of my "trebuchet" delivery. Silver Billy let out a loud yelp as he dropped his bat and began to hop about clutching the toes upon his left foot. "No ball, no ball," cried out the opposing team as they ran out onto the field to gather around their man.

"No ball", echoed the umpires belatedly as they too joined the growing throng around the now prostrate Silver Billy whilst Mr John Fenton came across to haul me from the pitch and dust me off.

"You have certainly started something now Henry."

Fists were shaken in my face with calls of "cheat" by the opposition supporters who now rushed to the wicket with the cheering home crowd in close pursuit, casting their hats into the air as they went. Amongst the confusion a coach and four left the London Road and rattled on across the turf to draw a halt beside the grand melee in the centre of the cricket field. A smartly attired gentleman stepped briskly from the coach whereupon he ordered the coachman to fire his blunderbuss into the air to quickly restore order and to quell this fervent assembly of cricketers, supporters and bookmakers. It appeared that the owner of Stonehenge Down was issuing a writ against all the participants of the cricket match which would be enforced forthwith unless this unauthorised activity ceased with immediate effect. The unpredictable Forth Marques of Queensbury had it seems not given his written consent for the match to take place much to the chagrin of our captain who claimed to have agreed the matter over dinner with the elderly Duke some months ago.

"I reminded him by letter only last week." He protested fruitlessly.

This unwelcome and unexpected news, delivered in stentorian tones by "Old Q's" official representative, had the effect of dousing the ardour of those who felt aggrieved by the outcome of the day for the cricket match and indeed the cricket field was no more. Orders were given for the wickets to be plucked from the turf and for the tents to be removed. Finally the two perplexed captains shook hands and it was agreed that a match should be played, at a mutually agreeable location, perhaps next year and the prize would be preserved until such time that a winning team could be determined. All wagers made were now declared null and void due to the unforeseen abandonment of the game and indeed it was this circumstance that caused the greatest discontent. Silver Billy was helped to his feet and I sincerely wished to apologise in person for my action but still I dared not make my approach for fear of reprisal by the opposition supporters and instead accepted a ride in a carriage to the George Inn.

My dear uncle, I cannot undo what I have done and I am indeed thankful that the game was halted and yet I do not believe that my heinous crime upon the cricket pitch shall be so readily forgot. As I sit at the writing desk in my room before the open window I can still hear the grumblings below in the yard as coaches are boarded.

"I believe gentlemen that we have been witness to the biggest travesty since Shock White arrived at the crease with his over–wide bat."

"I agree Sir, a travesty of equal proportions. Let us hope and pray that we never again witness the over-arm ball."

*

My dear uncle, I had no sooner completed my account of the day when there was a knock upon the door and boots announced that Mrs Mary Cunnington wished to speak to me in the parlour. Boots assured me that all cricketers and their supporters had now departed the George Inn and I found all to be quiet in the smoke filled parlour with the exception of Mrs Mary Cunnington who coughed before speaking.

"Henry, would you care to accompany us to the River Avon as Ann intends to go angling this evening?"

I replied that I should welcome the opportunity for I had never before witnessed the catching of a fish.

"Then shall we depart for there is a short walk to be taken?"

Ann awaited us in the courtyard where she held upright a long hazel wand with a number of wire hoops bound along its length and also a spool attached at the thicker end.

"Henry, please would you carry the rod and the net,

there is also a small bag. I am so very fond of fishing that
I insisted that I must bring my rod to Amesbury and papa
has arranged with the farmer that I may try the river at
Ratfyn."

As we walked from the town and made our approach
to the River Avon, I enquired of the day's barrow openings
for I was keen to establish whether there had been further
astounding discoveries amongst the Stonehenge barrows.
Miss Ann Cunnington explained that it appeared that the
examined barrows had already received the attention of the
tomb robber and therefore any content had been extracted
and the information lost to the enquiry.

"We believed this to be possible at the outset but Sir
Richard requires of papa that we must be most thorough in
our investigations."

It was now Ann's turn to question me upon the events of
my day and as I carefully considered my words, Mrs Mary
Cunnington interjected;

"It is a curious game that shows men to be boys at
heart."

"Mama, please," Admonished her daughter quickly as
she reddened and looked away.

I apologised for not knowing that they had indeed
observed the game upon Stonehenge Down for I should
have wished to attend to their comfort there.

"We walked across from the barrow opening.."
explained Mrs Mary Cunnington, "..and found it to be a

very noisy affair."

"You were occupied with the bat in your hand Henry and we wished to return to assist my father..for that is our purpose here this week, is it not mama?"

We continued in silence until we met with the river where our silence became more comfortable as stealth is indeed a requirement for the successful angler.

"Mama, you can sit there.." ordered her daughter in a whisper "..and Henry and I will cross the hatches and return downriver for a short distance."

Ann instructed me quietly that it was important to observe the activity upon the river before we commenced. I knew not what I should be observing and soon succumbed to the gentle gliding motion of the water as it passed before us. I could sense no discernable gradient to determine in which direction it should flow but the river appeared certain enough of its origin and destination for there to be any confusion over the matter. A large ripple upon the calm surface of the river betrayed the position of a fish and also the nature of the fly upon which it was happy to take its evening meal.

"Can you see the fly Henry? There are blue winged olives aplenty this evening."

Indeed I could now detect the curious movement of these flies as they jigged up and down and Ann was soon rummaging in her bag for a feathery imitation of this species that was bound together with a small barbed hook.

This keen young angler spent a moment affixing the fly to the final short length of fine silk thread and explained that the remainder of the line upon the spool is of a weightier waxed silk to enable it to be cast through the air.

Ann now raised herself to stand beside me upon the bank and having released a generous length of thread from the spool then flicked the supple hazel wand back and forth to enable the fly to arc repeatedly above the river. Once she was satisfied with her aim this feathery deceit dropped discreetly upon the surface to float gently towards the position of the fish. From his watery world the hungry creature quickly inspected this fresh arrival but then ignored the invitation. The fly was impatiently whisked away and after a further swishing through the air it once more landed gracefully upon the water and on this occasion the temptation proved too great. With the rod bending and line quivering in the hands of Miss Ann Cunnington the ensnared fish fled downstream taking with it a deal of thread from the unwinding spool. With a firm stance upon the bank the young angler lifted the hazel rod to retrieve the fish after its flight and by winding the thread upon the spool the resisting weight attached to the hook was drawn ever closer.

"Henry, the net."

I was able to just reach the struggling shape with the hooped net without myself entering the water and lifted out the weighty fish where it fought hard against this unwelcome exposure.

"Take the priest." Ann Cunnington then laughed out loud at the expression upon my face to this curious demand as she gestured to a heavy short wooden stick that had been placed upon the bank in readiness.

"It is so called for it serves the last rites. Strike upon the back of the neck and then remove the hook. It is a fine trout."

I was not prepared for my complicity in this struggle but as instructed I carried out this most un-priestly act. After Ann reached down to remove the hook from the fishy lip the creature inexplicably came back to life and quickly wriggled from my grasp to bounce from the grassy bank into the shallow waters where it made its escape.

"Henry!"

From across the river Mrs Mary Cunnington looked up from her book at the sound of her daughter's raised voice and smiled before settling back comfortably against a tree with the book now closed upon her lap.

"Let us try again Henry, and this time you may cast the fly and if you are successful then I shall ensure that the fish is thoroughly dealt with."

We walked a few paces further upstream until a new fish betrayed it's presence by disturbing the placid surface. Ann ordered me to stand beside her and she demonstrated how I must hold the rod and I practised the necessary flick with the hazel wand before attempting to cast the fly to the water. All was set and I made my cast but knew not where the fly and hook had gone.

"You have made a catch Henry…" Ann covered her mouth as she laughed, "…you have caught your hat."

I hastily removed the snakecatcher's hat and Ann carefully drew the hook from the desiccated snake hat band.

"It is a very curious hat Henry..and very old. I should like to accompany you to the gentleman's clothiers so that you may purchase a new hat."

Until today I had not experienced this close proximity with a young woman since that night in Hindon where Miss Sarah Foster and I first met and circumstances dictated that we should conceal ourselves in a stationary carriage.

With the fishing rod now placed out of harm's way upon the bank we sat and observed the fish as they fed safely upon the unwitting fly as nature had intended and without our wily interference.

"Henry, you are young, as I am young..but are you now betrothed..for I have heard it said that you are?"

Of a sudden life all about the river paused, as birds perched and insects settled, the mammals ceased their activity in their bankside holes and the fish took no advantage of an easy morsel. In this complete stillness I awaited my own response to this most private of questions.

"I have indeed met..someone..and we correspond freely, but we have not yet openly pledged our troth.."

"But your correspondence..is through another? It cannot therefore be..intimate?"

I swallowed and reddened at this close quarter and questioning.

"We are able to exchange..our feelings."

"And those feelings..are they love?"

Ann turned to face me as if to demonstrate that looks alone could be sufficient in the conveyance of such a delicate subject. Indeed, I construed by this intimation that if there were not this facility then there must be some failure or fault when eyes cannot meet and words must be spoken. I broke her gaze and as might a cautious fish, I drew back from taking the fly and changed my course entirely to find a deep sunlit pool where no barb may reach me. After a lengthy pause I cast a handful of bankside soil into the water and introduced a new subject for discussion to break the thread of a young woman's curiosity. Ann turned to observe this scattered interruption to the pristine surface whilst I proposed that the river before us was perhaps the receptacle for the ancient generations, when all but the Kings and Queens were buried in their prominent barrows.

Miss Ann Cunnington's brow soon puckered at this distraction.

"Pray explain yourself?"

This abrupt change in her daughter's tone caused Mrs Mary Cunnington to waken from her brief slumber and lift the book from her lap to continue with her reading.

It is a notion that had not fully formed in my own mind but occurred whilst floating down this same river on Sunday afternoon. I reached down with my cupped hand to gather a small portion of the river and held it up before letting it trickle gently between my fingers.

"Observe the past, the present and the future.."

Ann continued to frown as the final droplets of water fell upon the bank.

"..this river is born of distant springs that shall one day meet the sea. In turn the rain quenches the earth for the crystal waters to rise again and emerge as the infant spring. Suppose, if you will, that ancient man had not yet discovered our god but instead believed in the ways of the earth upon which his life depended; The changing seasons, the fruits of nature, the power of fire and the eternal river. By committing their dead to this eternal flow, the spirits of the ancestors shall join the spirits of the bountiful earth to become one inextricable tale."

Ann now visibly recoiled as she gathered her bag.

"Mama, we are leaving. Mr Chalk I do not like your ideas for the rivers would be thick with bodies and it would be revolting and please do not offend further by insulting the Almighty."

I cast a further handful of fine dirt into the water to confirm in my own mind that a pot of ashes would disperse well enough.

"Are you to remain here depositing soil into the river or

will you now carry my rod?"

We returned in silence to the George Inn under a reddening early autumn sky with nothing to show for our labours beside the River Avon.

I wish you goodnight my dear uncle and I hope to dream of one whom I love dearly and who may indeed tolerate my idle thoughts.

Your wily Nephew,
HENRY CHALK

Wednesday morning 7th September 1808

M Y   D E A R   U N C L E ,

All has changed and I am very soon to depart for Salisbury and I inform you now Sir in the event of you corresponding when I have already vacated this place. Indeed I received two letters this morning and I hoped in vain that you might have broken your silence but I found it instead to be a prosaic enquiry from Mr Gerrity at Chalk's Brewery. The second letter was a brief note from Mr Robert Foster to confirm the time that he and Miss Sarah Foster shall be arriving in Salisbury on Saturday 10th of September.

I awoke this morning with my stomach reminding me that I had forsaken dinner in favour of our angling excursion and I therefore sought to break my fast at the earliest opportunity. Mr Philip Crocker was already prepared for the day and he enquired of the events of yesterday upon Stonehenge Down and I believe that he enjoyed my account of the game of cricket with all its twists and turns.

"Poor Mr William Beldham. David has slain Goliath upon Stonehenge Down, with a trebuchet rather than a slingshot."

Mr Crocker asked how I was able to perform with the

bat when I had not before ventured onto a cricket pitch. I described my roving about the ploughed fields in search of fashioned flint for I have the habit of striking away each discarded flint with my thumbstick once I have established that the piece has no merit to my investigation. Indeed my stick is pecked by these repeated blows and I seldom fail in sending these odd shaped stones spinning away to all quarters. A hazel stick is narrow and the flint often small whereas a cricket bat is broad and a ball is the size of a fist.

"There are many facets to your study of flint Henry, yet this is surely the most fortuitous and unexpected."

Having completed our repast and with the downstairs of the George Inn now a busy place, Mr Crocker suggested that we took the morning air to which I was happy to oblige. I soon confided in Mr Crocker that last evening I had accompanied Mrs Mary Cunnington and her daughter Ann who was keen to fish upon the river and that upon our excursion I was somewhat surprised by Miss Cunnington's curiosity regarding my own affairs and I knew not what to make of it. Mr Crocker halted and rubbed his chin thoughtfully.

"Henry, these are modern young ladies and they speak their mind and ask questions freely and directly. Ann is the youngest of the three daughters and is indeed the most precocious."

Mr Crocker looked about him lest there should be some danger of being overheard by the hedgerow and to be doubly certain he lowered his voice.

"I have the trust of this fine family for they are indeed my very dear friends and so I implore you to observe the utmost discretion with what I am about to tell you."

I assured Mr Crocker that this would be so as I am certain, my dear uncle, that you will not divulge these words to another living soul.

"Henry, it was Ann who proposed to her father that you might welcome a visit to Stonehenge Down to assist with the barrow opening. Mr Cunnington thought it an excellent suggestion in recognition of your genuine interest in antiquarian matters and so wrote to you upon that subject."

I confided in Mr Crocker, who has by this circumstance shown himself to be a true friend, that whilst Miss Ann Cunnington is both lively and interesting and indeed dedicated to her father's investigations, the course of my future is set and shall suffer no distraction. After a short silence between us I reached beneath my shirt and drew the fine silver chain above my collar that secured the dark flint heart in its mount of silver and displayed the piece to Mr Philip Crocker. I explained that at my request Mr Henry Shorto, who was a cutler in the city of Salisbury, had made an identical pair and Mr Crocker studied closely the fine workmanship and stated that he had not before considered that this common stone may be so beautiful. I informed him that in three days time the two flint hearts will again be reunited back in their place of origin whereupon Mr Crocker smiled and shook my hand warmly after he had digested the meaning of my statement. My companion's expression soon changed to one of concern when I stated that my plans had been thrown into confusion by the nature of our conversation and that it was now my intention to depart at once for Salisbury. I also explained that upon arriving I would again seek out my friend Mr Henry Shorto for I believed that we held a mutual interest in the ubiquitous flint of this County and there was still much to discuss upon this matter since our first encounter in May of this year.

On our return to the inn I sought out Mr William Cunnington to explain that it was necessary for me to leave their company and depart for Salisbury and I apologised for this unexpected news. I thanked Mr Cunnington sincerely for the invitation to attend this latest campaign upon Stonehenge Down and that I was truly fortunate to be present at the conquering of Bush Barrow for that was indeed a most memorable occasion. After they had completed their breakfast I also thanked Mrs Mary Cunnington and her daughter Ann who stated that I was unlikely to ever become an angler to which I readily concurred. Ann then displayed less warmth in her dealings with me than hitherto and bid me a curt farewell. Mr Philip Crocker shook my hand firmly but with a look of consternation upon his face and Mr John Fenton appeared in the parlour to announce that he was to accompany me upon the coach to Salisbury. I explained that as an ardent pedestrian it was my intention to walk to Salisbury and not to travel upon the coach at all whereupon Mr John Fenton looked aghast at this prospect and shot glances in all directions for guidance upon the matter. I believe that my sudden change of plan has caused some hasty consultation between Mr William Cunnington and Mr John Fenton to ensure that I should again be cosseted and kept safe from undisclosed dangers. As a consequence my preferred means of travel has been entirely overlooked and Mr John Fenton is now to become a pedestrian tourist and once he has finally prepared himself, then we shall depart.

Sir, I shall communicate again when I arrive at Salisbury.

Your troublesome Nephew
HENRY CHALK

Wednesday evening

MY DEAR UNCLE,

I should be much aggrieved with you and earlier in the afternoon this was indeed the case. I now regret deeply the thoughts that I held towards you for I since understand the circumstances by which you have deemed it necessary to publish my letters. I cannot describe the utter and profound shock of holding in my hand not one, but two books of my published correspondence to you; "A Tour in Search of Chalk" and "A Tour in Search of Flint". These small volumes were purchased in boards from a bookseller in Salisbury and they now sit before me upon Mr Henry Shorto's desk in his house in Rollestone Street.

Each idle thought and whim and indeed each expression of the love that I hold for another is now laid bare and I stand naked before the world. Shall the words I now write be themselves caught, bound and presented as A Tour in Search of Gold? Or indeed A Tour in Search of My Father's Soul?

Within the second volume entitled "A Tour in Search of Flint" I have read your "Letter to the Editor" and therein exists the sorry tale of a conspiracy held against you by those whom I had previously considered to be my friends. To know that you have written to your wayward nephew only for this correspondence to be withheld pains me greatly and I now sincerely wish to undo this injustice for you are my only living relative.

To publish all Sir is to court disaster, for that is the circumstance that has most literally been so narrowly averted here in Salisbury upon this very afternoon but it has led to the abrupt departure of Mr John Fenton from my company. Sir, I shall explain in due course but I have sought the assistance of Mr Henry Shorto who greeted me in his cutler's shop as a dear friend and I am very pleased to again make his acquaintance. Mr Shorto was most insistent that whilst I remained in Salisbury then I should do so as his guest for his young family are away at Basingstoke for a number of days and he is not at all accustomed to an empty house.

Whilst my host is unavoidably detained this evening on Society business, I have the opportunity of recording the events of this most extraordinary and unsettling day.

I shall not bore you with the full litany of Mr John Fenton's complaints as we made our slow progress from Amesbury for my walking companion was not equipped with a pack but instead a green bag that has been borrowed from Mrs Cunnington. After exchanging this bag from hand to hand he very soon tired of carrying it at all and then deposited it heavily upon the road with a cry of exasperation;

"Henry, this is intolerable."

In truth I craved my own company and would happily proceed on my own but I took pity upon my companion for the quandary of his obligation was writ large across his face. I offered to hold one handle of the bag whilst he took the other and in this curious manner we moved incrementally along the Avon valley. In time we made our way to higher ground whereupon Mr John Fenton cursed the interminable sheep flocks and the barren wastes before grumbling that he was now hungry. Without divulging my

intentions I directed our course not to Salisbury but instead
to the midst of Grovelly Wood and to the small domain of
Peter Winter the charcoal burner and his boy Tam. Not one
year ago I was shown great kindness by the charcoal burner
and I wished to visit them again in their smoke filled world.
We crossed the river Wylye at the village of Great Wishford
and upon ascending the downs we encountered many souls
carrying great faggots of brushwood back to their cottages
for it seems they are entitled to enjoy the largesse of the
great sprawling wood that sits atop the ridge.

John Fenton had exhausted all complaints and now
walked meekly beside me and made no comment as we
entered Grovelly Wood. I knew not the path that we should
take and so followed a course that I hoped would lead in
time to the ranging southern hazel coppices. We crossed a
broad central drive and in time the taller trees gave way
to a great succession of uncut and identical bushes and
amongst these we followed a web of faint paths. A breeze
rattled gently at the hazel leaves and brought notice of the
smouldering combustion of the charcoal industry and we
met with one charcoal burner at his work who upon hearing
the name Peter Winter nodded and gestured to a path as
though it were a thoroughfare in a busy city. The way ahead
proved to be little more than an entrance to a further maze
of flourishing hazel bushes and we soon became lost for I
knew not which direction we should take. We halted to rest
awhile and John queried whether it was ever our intention

to visit Salisbury and complained bitterly that we had not
a scrap of food to eat. I stooped to retrieve a freshly fallen
hazel nut and my companion looked on in disgust as I
broke open its shell with my teeth and offered the nut to
be eaten.

"Henry, if I were a pig I might consider it."

With not a cracked twig to betray their approach we
were taken aback as a band of gaunt and hollow eyed
nutters drifted silently before us through the low wood as
if they were weightless spirits bound only to this earth by
the ballast of their laden sacks. As the last spectral figure
vanished between the stands of hazel John dropped to the
woodland floor and looked aghast.

"Henry that shall soon be us if we do not find our way."

I urged John to get to his feet for I considered it my duty
to distribute some coins to assist these souls in securing
food and lodging for I believed them to be itinerants and
not local men. As we lumbered in pursuit of these ethereal
figures, no sooner had we found our way to a woodland track
then we encountered a small but imposing figure standing
in our path. I soon recognised it to be Peter Winter the
charcoal burner and I was much relieved to again make
his acquaintance but did not receive the greeting that I
expected. A dark storm quickly gathered upon this little
man's furrowed brow and before I could speak he flew at
me causing John Fenton to hastily come between us. I have
described before the impediment to the charcoal burner's

speech whilst he strained to be understood and was clearly
in a condition of great anxiety but I could not comprehend
the woodman's plight. Without warning he turned about
and urged us to follow and we were barely able to keep
pace whilst I caught sight of the band of emaciated
nutters passing from our view upon a different trail and
I much regretted not being able to come to their aid. In
time we reached an encampment where I fully expected
to find the boy Tam and the mention of the boy's name
only served to agitate the man further as he rummaged in
his crude shelter. The encampment was not as before for
it had moved to a new grove amongst recently cut hazel
bushes and a great orderly clamp of wood was stacked and
prepared for the making of charcoal but was not yet lit.
Peter Winter returned with the book Treasure Island, as he
had done at our first encounter but he did not wish me to
read from the book and instead waved it in the air whilst
pointing at me and grunting in frustration. I knew that Tam
lay at the heart of this mystery and as I spoke his name
again the little man nodded wildly and pointed away into
the wood as if directing us to the boy. To alarm us further
he then pretended to cast a noose around his own neck and
mimicked the death throes of a hanged man. Peter Winter
threw the old book to the forest floor and again urgently
beckoned us to follow him and at a trot we took a woodland
trail until a broad track was met and in time we emerged
from the wood where a distant view of Salisbury Cathedral

now lay before us. There was no mistaking our destination for the charcoal burner grunted and pointed to the slender spire and chased us down the track for a short distance to hurry us on our way to Salisbury.

As we descended towards Wilton I breathlessly recounted to John Fenton the circumstance of witnessing the apportioning of a stolen deer at the New Inn and young Tam's complicity in that illegal act. John's lethargy and resentment at his enforced pedestrianism was now replaced by a growing curiosity and he stated that perhaps the boy had again engaged in this illicit activity and was now residing in the gaol as a consequence. At the Bell Inn we were fortunate that a Salisbury bound coach was soon to depart and as three passengers had disembarked to visit Wilton House we were able to secure inside seats. John Fenton and I sat with our luggage beside us to enable a hasty exit at the Gaol as agreed with the coachman upon pressing two shillings into his hand. We travelled in silence but all the while my head span as I speculated upon the awful circumstances that might lie before us. At the dread building that is Fisherton Gaol we were met with blank expressions when I enquired of the boy Tam, for we had no surname to offer. John Fenton soon pushed me aside.

"Gateman, we wish to know the fate of the young poacher who took a deer from the wood at Wilton, by name of Tam."

This blunt demand did indeed meet with the

acknowledgement that the boy's name was Thomas Targett and not Tam at all and I have again been fooled by the vagaries of the Wiltshire tongue. Upon the release of another coin the gateman revealed that the boy was this very day at the Petty Sessions where with two further men they shall stand before the magistrate. Through the streets of Salisbury we dashed to the new Council House where the Usher informed us that the Court had broken for luncheon and would resume upon the return of the Magistrate. The official confirmed that Thomas Targett and the two men would appear before the bench this afternoon and added that their case was "Pecu'lar" in that the case against the accused had been established by evidence contained within a book. I pressed the man to inform as to which book could possibly relate such a tale at which he rubbed his chin.

"'Tis a Tur in Zarch o' Chalk boi A Pudestrin' or zummat."

At first I could by no means comprehend the gravity of this disclosure and I enquired whether this book was on sale within the City.

"Oi believes zo yus zur."

The official closed the door upon us and whilst John Fenton continued to question the relevance of a book to this case, a cold fear soon overwhelmed me and I tried to gather my thoughts.

"John, I know not how it has come to pass but I sincerely

believe that it is a book that I have inadvertently written
and it is my own words that condemn young Thomas Targett
and the two men."

I confirmed that this also explained the behaviour of
the charcoal burner for he had gesticulated towards me
with a book in a most accusing manner. John burst out
laughing at my words as he believed it a preposterous
notion that one could write a book without knowing of it.

"Let us go to the booksellers Henry to find your
mysterious book."

After visiting three books sellers with John Fenton
mimicking the Court Usher by requesting "A Tur in
Zarch O'Chalk boi A Pudestrin'" and receiving nothing
but puzzled expressions, upon the forth attempt, to my
great astonishment, we were successful. The bookseller
presented us with a book in boards and my mouth was
agape as I read its label;

"A Tour in Search of Chalk through parts of South
Wiltshire in 1807 written in a series of letters by A
Pedestrian."

The bookseller queried whether we required both
books by the same author and before my eyes appeared
not one but two books of my pedestrian adventures. As you
well know my dear uncle the second volume is entitled "A
Tour in Search of Flint through parts of South Wiltshire in
1808."

"Henry, you have been busy. Give me your purse, we

shall take both books."

John demanded that we required fortification after this discovery and led me to the Plume of Feathers in Queen Street and soon placed a large brandy in my hands.

"You are certainly a dark horse Mr Chalk, or should I say Mr A Pedestrian. We must however think clearly and act quickly if we are to help the boy. Where in these books are the words that incriminate young Thomas Targett?"

I could not at first bare to touch these books and instead stated that it must be recorded towards the fore of the first volume where I endured the hospitality of the reprehensible New Inn and it was the night that I left my bed and chose instead to sleep amongst the straw above a stable. As John flicked through the pages of "A Tour in Search of Chalk" he at first confirmed that it was you Sir who had initiated the publication of my private letters and I confess my anger grew with this revelation. John calmed me and stated that the most pressing business was to prepare a defence and my whimpering was not helping matters. I know not how long I sat staring blankly ahead before John slammed the book down upon the table making me jolt from my unpleasant reverie.

"This is what we must do. Henry you shall not appear at the court at all and you must place your faith in me. Until I return, under no circumstances, must you stray from this place and please will you now give me your word that this will be so?"

I muttered into my brandy that I would remain for I felt too shaken to do otherwise. Invigorated by a further brandy and the intrigue of the occasion John Fenton snatched up "A Tour in Search of Chalk" and was gone in a trice whilst I stared at the remaining volume. I was at first unable to touch the book as if it were the most vile object but curiosity and perhaps vanity overcame me and with trepidation I opened the bare boards. Upon reading the letter to the Editor, in your own words, it at once became clear your purpose in publishing my letters and indeed you knew that one day I would hold these books in my hand and that your efforts would overcome those who wished to keep us apart. I believed that you may have abandoned your Nephew and I cannot express enough my feelings of relief to find out that this is not so. My rage turned upon those so called guardians who purport to protect me from unforeseen dangers and from my own recklessness and surely Mr John Fenton forms part of this conspiracy. Despite any assurances to the contrary, for the circumstances had truly changed with this revelation, I arranged for our luggage to remain at the Plume of Feathers and hastened to the Courtroom where the afternoon session had already commenced.

I was fortunate that there was sufficient interest in this case to attract a decent public audience in the gallery and I kept myself secreted behind two taller gentlemen. Thomas Target looked pale and wide eyed as he peered from the dock, flanked by the Landlord of the New Inn and the man I once recorded as "Stoopid Martin". The Magistrate, one Mr Peter Maxfield Esq, was large and florid and scowled down at the accused as if their very presence in his court was sufficient to confirm their guilt. The crowd about me coughed, shuffled and muttered until the Magistrate lost patience and roared at the top of his voice;

"SILENCE. I must have silence or I shall throw you all out into the street where you belong. Pray excuse me, I do not direct this at you Mr Ramage, Miss Davies or you Mr Sheldrake."

The Magistrate now asked for the bookseller's assistant who had brought this case before the Court to be sworn in, whereupon the Usher thrust a bible towards this overtly expectant witness and he duly swore an oath.

"Tell the Court your name Sir."

"'Olford yer wurship"

"That would be Holford?"

"Indeed t'wud yer wurship."

"And you are in the employment of Brodie's the booksellers in the City of Salisbury?"

"I most zertainly is yer wurship."

"And you present as evidence for the offence of deer stealing by the accused who stand before us, a book entitled..A Tour in Search of Chalk, by A Pedestrian?"

"I does yer wurship. Turrible doings."

"Mr Holford, will you refrain from rubbing your hands

together whilst you address the court as it is most unseemly and one might argue that it is the author of this work who has recorded the crime and not yourself that may be due the financial gain of one third of the penalty."

"Ah, but ee ain't ere an' I is yer wurship."

With this exchange I shrank down further in my concealment for I did not wish to catch Tom Targett's or the Landlord's eye for any recognition would spell disaster. I could not as yet see John Fenton's position in the court.

The Magistrate continued to question the bookseller's assistant.

"Do you read all the books that you sell Mr Holford?"

"I dun't read zo good zur. Twas a cust'mer did tell I n' I is only doin' me duty yer wurship."

"Usher, will you now read the relevant sections of this book to the court."

The Usher now leant forward to whisper to the Magistrate.

"No you certainly may not borrow my spectacles. I shall read it myself."

I felt sick to the pit of my stomach as the courtroom now resounded with my own condemning words and the accused looked at one another in expressions of dread horror as their secretive exploits were broadcast by the Magistrate.

"As the court will now be aware, these most serious events also record the complicity of the Constable himself but I have been informed that he is since deceased."

The Magistrate now turned to address the three accused who all looked down at their feet rather than catch his eye.

"This deplorable act is clearly beyond the powers of this court for it requires the severest of sentences and I hold no doubt that transportation awaits you. You shall therefore remain in Fisherton Gaol until the October Assizes."

The Magistrate was poised with gavel in hand when I heard John Fenton's voice.

"Sir, please excuse me."

"What is this?"

"I have evidence pertinent to this case which may prevent a grave injustice here today. I am a good friend of Sir Richard Colt Hoare who is perhaps known to you?"

"Indeed he is, he is also a Magistrate..but you must be sworn in and give your name Sir, this is not a gentleman's club but a court of law."

John Fenton was duly sworn in and adopting his father's theatrical and stentorian tones he declared that until his arrival in Salisbury not one hour ago he had no knowledge of the existence of the book in question.

"I have made a cursory perusal and that is sufficient."

He then held up the first of the pair of books that we had just purchased and turned full circle to display the volume to all present within the court whilst I cowered down in my concealed position.

"I too appear in "A Tour in Search of Chalk". I shall

not however be seeking recourse for the slights against my character contained therein. It is well known to the literate public that modest works such as this are but a vain accomplishment and a concoction plagiarised from the work of real travellers and real authors. It is perhaps the only shred of truth within the book where my own father, Mr Richard Fenton, who is himself a lawyer and dear friend to Sir Richard Colt Hoare, upon page one hundred and sixty seven, makes the following statement and I read; " You travel, you correspond, you embellish and then you publish". My Father is currently concocting just such a work for his own amusement. It shall differ in that it will grandly entertain and it is to be called "A Tour in Quest of Genealogy". Indeed you may call it a satire upon such inferior works as the laborious scribbles of Mr A Pedestrian."

Once again my book was displayed to the court, as John Fenton paused in his delivery.

"Travel as we all know is tedium. Pedestrian travel is tedium in the extreme, Sir, I know for I have suffered it myself, though not of my own choosing. Any flight of fancy or ripe anecdote from some adventurous tale will enrich the piece and indeed the printing presses in Paternoster Row are a blur of ink and machinery and the bookstands in the Capital are creaking under the very weight of such vapid publications.

I now give an example that shall put beyond all doubt

the validity of this work as a faithful record of events. Sir, you will no doubt be familiar with the name..Mr William Beckford of Fonthill and that it is well known that he will admit no persons to his Abbey."

"I have heard it said.." agreed the Magistrate "..although it is the last place on earth that I should wish to visit and the last person on earth whom I should wish to encounter. The man is a fiend and an abomination, proceed Mr Fenton."

"Quite so Sir. Nevertheless the young pedestrian purports to have entered the forbidden grounds belonging to the "Abbott" of Fonthill..yes It is a nomenclature that our mutual friend the Baronet also finds amusing. He then enters the building, meets Mr William Beckford, ascends the tower and flees with a pack of slavering dogs at his heals. It is the fare of a limited imagination. Sir, it was I who made a wager of five guineas with the author that he should carry out this trespass. It was conducted as a consequence of much libation but hands were shaken and a wager is a wager after all."

"Indeed it is, pray continue."

"It was perhaps three days after the wager was set that I met again with the author whereupon, in the presence of Sir Richard Colt Hoare at his home in Stourhead, we listened to an admission of his failure to fulfil the terms of the wager. Sir, if you study the volume before you, and we have to endure one hundred pages until the account is given, of how our Pedestrian then claims to have succeeded in his mission to ascend the tower of Fonthill Abbey. I shall gladly request of Sir Richard Colt Hoare that he fully endorses my account, if it is the wish of the Court."

The Magistrate stated that he would not wish the Baronet to be troubled by such matters.

"Sir I should like to conclude that the incident of deer stealing is no less a fabrication than the entering of the domain of Mr William Beckford. It is a fine example of the embellishment recommended by my own father. It shall give colour to a bloodless tale for who wishes to read of the padding feet of a timid pedestrian and that Sir, is all I have to say on the matter."

"Mr Fenton, the Court has, I believe, established that the anonymous author is known to you?"

"He is Sir, but he is also an acquaintance of Sir Richard Colt Hoare and I would not wish to further sully the name of our noble friend by revealing such unfortunate.... connections. Indeed it would be best for all concerned if the remaining stock of this inferior work were to be destroyed to avoid any future indiscretions. I shall recommend this action to the author when we next meet."

"Quite so, quite so." Declared the magistrate before scowling again at the accused.

"Hmm, I do not doubt that these two men and that boy have it in them to commit such deeds for one only has to look at them. Tut tut..Their day shall surely come. I am very grateful to you Mr Fenton for your timely intervention.

The book is poorly writ. Case dismissed."

As the Magistrate banged his gavel upon the bench he again raised his voice.

"We are not yet finished. There is a question of costs. Mr Holford, will you stand?"

The bookseller's assistant now rose slowly to his feet with his shoulders drooping as he glowered across the Court towards the victorious John Fenton.

"Mr Holford, in bringing this most insubstantial case before the court you shall pay five shillings."

I rushed from the gallery for I sincerely wished to explain and apologise to Thomas Targett and the two men for the great trouble that I had caused but found only John Fenton strolling proudly from the Court and he turned sharply as I called out to him.

"John, where are Thomas and the two men?"

John Fenton dismissed my question and instead berated me loudly for not remaining as I had promised at the Plume of Feathers. I informed him that I could not care less what he thought and my concerns were for the accused men and the boy Tom.

"They have fled Henry for caged foxes require little encouragement to bolt for freedom. I have averted disaster here today and yet you do not thank me?"

I could not however contain my rage and declared my abhorrence at witnessing John Fenton's pleasure in the condemning of my words and most private thoughts at which he protested most vehemently.

"I have done today what all good lawyers do. I have said what needed to be said and without falsehood. I wished to spare you any public humiliation hence extracting beforehand your sincere promise that you would remain at the Inn. You did not do so you and have brought this pathetic and ungrateful indignation upon yourself. I am shot through the heart and shall return immediately to Pembrokeshire. You can meet with whom you like at Salisbury cathedral and your friendly cutler, Mr Henry Shorto can guard over you for I am done with trying to help Henry Chalk. I am very hungry and where is my wretched bag?"

I informed John Fenton that his bag was safe at the Plume of Feathers whereupon he swiftly turned on his heel and left me standing outside the Council House. I now realise that even Mr Philip Crocker has broken my confidence as I have told no person other than he of my plans to meet with Mr Henry Shorto. Mr Crocker has related the details of our private conversation to John Fenton and it seems that none can be trusted whom I once considered to be my friends. No persons have been informed either of my meeting with Robert and Sarah Foster at Salisbury Cathedral and so Mr John Fenton has surpassed himself in the reading of my correspondence at the George Inn this morning. Perhaps whilst I walked with Mr Crocker, Mr John Fenton was in my room reading my private papers. What is private now my dear uncle?

Mr Henry Shorto has no such allegiances and has just returned home therefore I now conclude my sorry tale for I have much to explain to one whom I may trust without reservation.

Your faithful Nephew,
HENRY CHALK

Thursday 8th September 1808

My dear Uncle,

Despite my comfortable bed I have had a restless night for I have been unable to stop my mind from churning over the events of yesterday. Last evening I explained to Mr Shorto all that has occurred and he thinks it a most extraordinary tale. Sir, I am now caused some embarrassment for my meeting with Mr Shorto in May of this year is also recorded in the second volume of my published letters and he has referred to my departure from his house in the early morning.

"I better understand your action Henry from the reading of these pages. At the time I confess to being greatly disappointed for there was much that I still wished to discuss."

This morning after studying me across the breakfast table he interrupted my reverie;

"There is a simple antidote for your condition Mr Chalk. My family are not due to return until Saturday, when you also have a meeting in Salisbury. I propose a short pedestrian excursion, not a grand tour but a modest ramble, once I ensure that there is no outstanding business that cannot await my return."

I could see that my host was barely able to conceal his excitement at the prospect of becoming a pedestrian tourist and so I welcomed this suggestion.

"Henry you are better associated with the world outside the boundary of this City than I. My old boots must suffice and I require a pack so if you will excuse me, I shall return as quickly as I am able."

Whilst Mr Shorto attends to his affairs I must inform you of an issue upon which my mind is already set. Sir, I invite and welcome you to join Chalk's Brewery as a partner and no longer will you be cast as a spectre in the shadows by those who do not know you. We shall go forth in business together and banish our estrangement for it is a circumstance that I cannot comprehend and one that I am now most fervently unwilling to perpetuate. Indeed when I gather my thoughts, I shall write to the trustees of Chalk's Brewery to insist upon this arrangement with instructions that it be carried out forthwith. I hope and prey that you will accept this proposal.

My dear uncle you have gone to the trouble and expense of publishing the accounts of my wanderings with the intention of ensuring our reunion. I do however remain aghast at the discovery that you have broadcast to the world my most private thoughts. When my letters went unanswered I did become less guarded in my words for it was as if I were writing only to myself. Indeed you are vindicated by your actions but others have read these books as I witnessed only yesterday in the Courtroom in Salisbury. I now also understand better the antics of the pedestrian tourist who found my spyglass upon the long barrow and put it to good use before returning it to me at the Winterslow Hut. I was at the time perplexed by his intimate knowledge of my previous ramblings but all is now explained for he possessed a copy of "A Tour in Search of Chalk" when I did not know that such a book existed. As I had become inspired by your book "A Pedestrian Tour of North Wales,1805" and so this fellow had decided to follow the course of my first pedestrian adventure. Sir, there are consequences that have already arisen and may yet arise from your actions. Before Mr Shorto returns I have perhaps one hour to visit each and every bookseller in Salisbury to purchase all remaining copies of these first and second volumes of my published letters for I intend to destroy them. They have served your purpose my dear uncle.

Your Nephew and forthcoming partner in business,
HENRY CHALK.

Thursday evening.

THE GLOVE INN

Mr Shorto and I did not leave Salisbury as early as we might but nevertheless have enjoyed a fine afternoon. We are this evening staying at the Glove Inn and you may recall that it is a place that I have visited before at the foot of Whitesheet Hill. It was not my intention to record the details of our excursion but Mr Shorto is now engaged in corresponding to an unsuspecting relation no doubt to inform of his new life as a pedestrian tourist. I warned my friend that he may soon find his words in print and so to manage his subjects well and with discretion.

There is always a pleasant expectancy when departing upon any ramble and today in Mr Shorto's company his eagerness was palpable but he assured me at the outset that he would not talk all the way.

In truth we did not exchange one word until we gained the elevation of the raceplain where we observed from a distance a noisy cluster of humanity and the bright colours of a race meeting soon to commence. Rather than gamble our money away, I directed Mr Shorto to a hazel bush beside the turnpike where I used his penknife, indeed a tool manufactured in his own workshop and with "Shorto Salisbury" stamped upon its blade, to cut a stick as befits a pedestrian tourist. I explained my preference for a stick not with a cleft at the top and instead it must be the thick end which should be held in the hand. The opposing and narrower end shall serve one better in all regards and I demonstrated to Mr Henry Shorto how with this whippy stick brambles and nettles may be severed at a blow whilst it is still stout enough to support the weight

of a man. This narrow end may prize out a buried flint for
inspection or test the depth of a bog before entering. It
shall poke, prod, push, scrape, slash or strike and once
broken it is easily replaced with another. An old dry stick
may preserve fond memories but a green stick will bring
vigour and I proclaimed it to be the weapon of choice for
the Pedestrian Tourist. In response Mr Shorto brandished
his new hazelstick as might a fencing master.

"En garde Monsieur Chalk."

Our sticks now clashed together as we engaged in
battle to the great amusement of an overflowing carriage
of passing racegoers who called out their encouragement.

From the lofty raceplain we followed the ghosts of the
the Roman Empire and you may find useful reference upon
page "L" in the second volume of my travails my dear
uncle for I am covering old ground.

There is a thread of life that has long existed in the
valley to the South of the raceplain with the gentle river
Ebble at its heart. The grand old church of Bishopstone
stands in near isolation for the new village of Bishopstone
has inexplicably moved away to a new location further up
the valley. The old village is but a series of humps and
bumps in a grass field and my walking companion paused
as we gazed out upon this conspicuous desertion.

"Where once the cottage stood, the hawthorn grew
Remembrance wakes, with all her busy train
Swells at my breast and turns the past to pain."

I complimented Mr Shorto on his recitation for such fine words along the way shall serve him well in his ambition to become a pedestrian tourist.

How perfect for the keeping of life is the crystal clear river Ebble? The mills and constructed meadows shall compete for its bounty, to push the paddles or to drown the fresh grass. As a consequence of a discussion with Mr Philip Crocker during my convalescence at Stourhead I now understand better this fine system where in the early months of the year the water shall protect the young grass in the meadows from the deadly frost. The water is encouraged to float down these slight gradients from the intricate raised channels thereby covering and protecting the nub of the grass root. It is the job of the "drowner" to work his meadow by blocking with a turf here or releasing the flow elsewhere. During the day the sheep may now feed upon this early season bite of grass and the shepherd will at night pen the flock upon the sides of the valley where they shall enrich the soil. The hazel hurdles that form these pens must be moved daily to ensure that each arable field enjoys its share of the "golden hoof".

My companion listened avidly and encouraged me to continue with this calendar of life outside the city walls.

"The ploughman turns the enriched soil and the sowers cast last harvest's seed; the boys rattle at the birds as the green shoots show and at the end of summer the harvesters bend their backs to bring in the prize to the satisfaction of the wealthy landowner. As winter steals the daylight hours the corn is threshed in the dusty barn and a weight of water is held back before the mill for the faithful river Ebble to again serve the landowner well.

The old mill splashes and rumbles into life with the rotation of paddles, gears and the grinding together of great millstones.

In addition to the refinement of a portion of the Squire's harvest many a smallholder would require the services of the mill and the cart or packhorse would make this journey upon paths and ways born out of necessity, bringing the corn and then grumbling home with the flour after begrudging the sly miller his dubious share of the smallholder's annual toil."

My walking companion considered this short account of rustic life.

"Imagine Henry if life in England beyond this horizon one day ceased altogether, could not this gentle valley continue as it always had and there would be enough for all?"

I stated that I should like to consider that this was once the way of it in simpler times but that now our entire globe shall be the new horizon. I explained that it was my ambition to export Chalk's Pale Ale far and wide across the continent in glass bottles but first the barley must come from somewhere, such as these cultivated slopes above the gentle river Ebble. My friend again considered the words of Mr Goldsmith:

> "A time there was, ere England's griefs began
> When every rood of ground maintain'd its man
> For him light labour spread her wholesome store
> Just gave what life required, but gave no more."

We had now drawn to a standstill as if walking and discussion were not compatible bedfellows and I encouraged my friend to bring his thoughts with him for we must make progress on our ramble.

There followed a lengthy silence as we climbed from the Ebble valley to gain a ridge to the South to follow a broad drover's path on our westerly course and I thought back to the cycle of life in the Ebble valley and also to a song that I heard the harvesters sing over and again upon the occasion of the harvest home at Widdington Farm. Now with breath to spare I gave voice to this song although I have had little experience of singing in company but as I completed the first few verses Mr Shorto listened intently and then joined in with the chorus with his rich and deep voice supporting the melody like the solid foundations of an old barn. The song is I believe called John Barleycorn and is in keeping with the suspicions and mystery bound up with the cutting of the last sheaf of the harvest and every means is taken to try to kill poor John Barleycorn but he returns with vigour and it is a blessing for without his sustenance we should surely ourselves die of hunger. John Barleycorn is now incarcerated within the great ricks across the land and despite the blades, forks and the beating with crabtree sticks before the eventual grinding between great stones that must always be perpetrated upon the poor fellow he shall survive. Mr Shorto paused to produce a penny loaf from his pack and we chewed upon a crust in celebration of John Barleycorn and once we had swallowed him we began the song again and so a brewer and a cutler idled away their afternoon in a pleasurable rhythm of song, conversation and observation.

In due course our progress was interrupted by the most extraordinary vista to the South of our ridge which caused us to stand in acceptance of the time required to explore the diminishing scale of fields, hedges, valleys and woods. A rising twist of smoke here and there flagged some degree of conflagration in a cottage hearth or woodland clearing but with the harvest now over we could detect little other human activity from our lofty perch. In regular formation a fleet of plump white clouds floated gently above this late summer mantle of the county of Dorsetshire and perhaps Hampshire also and in the far distance the sea glistened like treasure laid out in the sun. I speculated that it must be the chalky cliffs of the Isle of Wight that we could discern beyond the shimmering sea and I lamented that I had not brought my spyglass for fear of mislaying it again. Our contemplation was disturbed by a large flock of sheep being driven towards our position and rather than become engulfed in livestock we were forced to stand aside. The surface of this way is pock marked by the hoof and we encountered two more great flocks of these horned sheep as we continued on our westerly course.

I now discouraged my friend from making an inspection of the views to our North until we had gained the highest elevation upon our ramble and I pointed ahead towards the clump of trees that was our goal.

"So Henry you had a purpose and a destination all along."

I explained that it was at this same clump of trees, in May of this year, that I had realised the loss of my spyglass for I saw it glinting from a distant long barrow. Upon reaching this vantage point I now cast my arm to the north where the dark and wooded undulations of the vale offer a broad interruption to the ubiquitous chalk ridges and plains of South Wiltshire. With the uniform chalk layer disturbed and removed by some distant upheaval it is a place of exposed rock, clay and water seepages where the River Nadder collects its sandy and snaking character before conforming to the rules of the river Avon beside Salisbury Cathedral. I advised my friend that as you wander the dark and deeply incised lanes of this mysterious vale the mischievous sprites of earth and stone shall dart about amongst the shadows and cause the visitor many a backward glance. Despite my best attempts to distract it was inevitably Mr Beckford's conspicuous tower standing upon its prominent elevation within the vale that drew my companion's attention.

"So there it is, Fonthill Abbey. Henry from what you tell me of Mr John Fenton's presentation in court, I know not whether you gained access to the tower and therefore the deer stealers were indeed guilty or whether all is embellishment and justice was fairly seen to be done by the two men and the boy?"

I stated that I chose not to answer his question and neither did I wish to approach the Abbey and from my answer he must draw his own conclusions.

Our stomachs informed us that we must soon eat and so we made our way towards the Glove Inn and skirted around the grounds of Ferne House lest I should again meet the daughter of that place.

Mr Shorto has now concluded his correspondence and so I must put down my pen for there is more to life than a perpetual record of one's existence.

*

Through Mr Shorto's vigilance and curiosity a mystery has been unearthed. My companion had opened Gulliver's Travels at an arbitrary place and it was the chapter from Gulliver's adventure in Laputa, the flying island. I had not yet progressed this far in the story and Mr Shorto chuckled to himself as he read but upon turning the page he paused.

"Henry, will you please show me again the curious

script in your father's hand?"

There was an urgency to this request not in keeping with the pensive nature of my walking companion and I swiftly did as he asked. Last night I had shared this mystery with my host explaining how my departure from Southwark was hastened by the discovery of this single sheet of paper inserted inside the book causing me to follow in my father's footsteps.

"Look here at this diagram on page one hundred and sixty two for it contains a multitude of squiggles and see how they compare with your father's script."

When the two pages were gathered before the candle there was indeed a similarity but I stated that there were many more characters in the table than were written upon the page. With a pen and paper he proceeded to try to make sense of this new conundrum but after a lengthy period he sighed and put down his pen.

"There must be some order to this Henry or perhaps our own alphabet is coded amongst this table but where to start?"

I now wondered at my father's denial that he possessed a copy of Gulliver's Travels and that it was not after all a fear that it may corrupt and offend but instead that it contained a greater mystery that he did not wish me to encounter. We must now sleep upon this puzzle and in the morning we shall venture forth into the dark vale.

*

AT WARDOUR CASTLE

A dense fog occurred in the night and greeted us as we strode away from the Glove Inn. I decided that we should seek out the long barrow, where I had before mislaid the spyglass and we soon left the turnpike and made our way up Whitesheet Hill. The fine mist clung to our clothes and caused the multitude of spider's webs to sag under this drenching and we still did not rise above the fog even with our clambering upon the ancient tomb at the crest of the ridge.

Mr Shorto requested the second published volume of my letters and upon extracting it from my pack I was about to speak when he smiled and held up his hand for me to remain silent.

"Here it is, page fourteen."

My friend read in silence for a short time and then closed the book.

"My dear A Pedestrian, it is one aspect of having your words and thoughts in print for you no longer have to repeat yourself. You suggest Henry that a chronology may be established and you have witnessed with your own eyes the fine and rare metals extracted from Bush Barrow, which you inform me is a round tomb. We must not forget that every past era had a past, present and a future and for these stone dependent peoples, who rest beneath our feet, the appearance of metal was beyond their horizon. One can only speculate at the arrival of the first metals, perhaps brought by strangers to our shores and indeed the occupant of Bush Barrow was fairly replete with metals and he may be adjudged to be a foreigner, a magician, a king or indeed the architect of Stonehenge itself such is the proximity of his tomb to the great stones from your description Henry.

To present a piece of gold to the occupants of our long barrow would indeed mystify but its softness renders it useless to a hunter or a rudimentary farmer. It is an adornment and its rarity still implies wealth and power today so I propose that the occupant of Bush Barrow is more of our world than that of his stone dependent ancestors."

I could but agree with the insight of a cutler for my companion offers a fresh and insightful view into the mysteries of the past and I suggested that he will one day make a fine antiquary.

The sun appeared to be in no hurry to assert itself but as we speculated upon the distant past a pale blue sky slowly emerged through the dying miasma to confirm that a fine day was in prospect. We followed the old abandoned turnpike in an easterly direction for a short distance before scaling down the grassy slopes of this ridge to cross the new road and in time passed under a rock arch to make our approach to Old Wardour Castle. Settled in its comfortable hollow there is sufficient misty light remaining to assist with the picturesque splendour of this ruin and my walking companion is now immovable from this spot and he draws whilst I write. I have before established that Mr Shorto is a fine draftsman and I have just interrupted him to make a compliment as his drawing nears completion.

"Drawing, painting, observing birds, poetry and now, since meeting you Mr Chalk, pedestrianism and a curiosity regarding flint. These are the subjects that preoccupy me whilst my trade is that of a cutler."

I shall now take the opportunity to study again my father's curious script and compare it to the table of squiggles in Gulliver's travels to see whether I can make any sense of it.

*

Friday evening

ROLLESTONE STREET, SALISBURY

So we are now returned to Rollestone Street and I can barely consider what tomorrow shall bring for Miss Sarah Foster arrives in Salisbury with her brother Robert. Mr Shorto has blisters on both feet and as he hobbled into the hallway he proudly displayed his hazel stick to the housekeeper who tutted about what Mrs Shorto would have to say on the matter.

We were required to ride on the outside of the coach from the village of Hindon to the Deptford Inn this afternoon and we there had two hours to wait before we secured seats aboard the Salisbury coach. We did not arrive at Mr Shorto's house until nine o clock and after a bath and a late supper I now dare not let my mind wander and so I shall conclude the tale of our ramble.

Mr Shorto has already proved that he will make a better pedestrian tourist than I for he recites poetry and is a splendid draughtsman and I believe in time will become a respected antiquarian. From old Wardour Castle we meandered towards the village of Tisbury which is surely an old habitation for it lies at the natural heart of a vale that appears as old as time itself. The church displays an ancient importance on its site beside the river Nadder and there is a hollow yew tree of extraordinary age and girth in the churchyard. There are many stone quarries in Tisbury and it is a trade that must depend upon the outlying web of small lanes for the twisting river is not navigable. The stone for Salisbury Cathedral has its origins in this quarter of South Wiltshire and the challenge of transporting such huge volumes of freestone before the advent of any turnpike road speaks of a powerful determination. A traveller in this County is able to view Wiltshire's rich geology displayed upright within the fabric of its village buildings and it is uniformly the very local materials that are torn from the valley sides, collected from the fields or dug from the ground that are gratefully utilised. Only the most ambitious undertakings demand the ostentation of imported materials

and Salisbury Cathedral and Stonehenge shall command
our respect and wonder in this regard.

In one small quarry I found a dark and glassy substance
that has the character of flint but is perhaps more course. I
have struck it and it breaks like flint and is sharp enough
to warrant the effort should there be no flint available.
Mr Shorto has retrieved a piece for he intends to make
a collection of flint to enable a study of its origins and
this substance is close enough in character to justify its
transportation back to Salisbury.

The lure of Fonthill Abbey gnawed away at my walking
companion and also guided his feet for in the airless late
morning we followed a brook from Tisbury in the direction
of Mr Beckford's domain. We soon found ourselves
entering a deep and narrow valley where the heavy ground
was slippery under foot for this is a place of many springs,
heavy clay and water seepages.

"Observe the alder tree Henry that prospers here and
the horsetails for they both require an abundance of water."

With Mr Henry Shorto by my side, every natural thing
that we encounter now has a name and I have learned
much from my companion. The burgeoning hedgerows
are becoming an untangled mystery for the ripe berries
of the briar are indeed pleasantly sweet to eat whilst
the sloe of the blackthorn is sour and unpleasant for Mr
Shorto playfully encouraged me to bite into this tempting
black fruit. Also the handsome butterfly that fortuitously

guided me to inspect Gulliver's Travels in my father's study is known as the Red Admiral, a summer visitor to these shores. I have explained the significance of this bright and fluttering creature to my friend and he suggests that I shall forever think on my father when I spy a Red Admiral on my travels.

"Butterflies are surely the greatest adornment of the English summer Henry and the Red Admiral is perhaps the most striking of all."

The hot sun bore down as we made our steady way up this windless and deeply incised valley and above the tree tops upon the near horizon small white clouds bubbled up as if we were immersed in a great frothing pot. A jay and then a green woodpecker passed noisy judgement before us, with first a screech of alarm to be seconded by the mocking laugh of the woodpecker as Fonthill Abbey again revealed itself. My stomach tightened with the memory of my clandestine visit to that place and I wished for some grand distraction to enable us to take a different course and forget entirely about Fonthill Abbey. The sprites of earth and stone kindly afforded my wish for in the most unlikely manner a distraction was stumbled upon. At a place where the infant brook wound through an open meadow we knelt beside the stream to splash cool water into our hot faces. My friend released the cupped water from his hands and from the bed of the shallow stream he removed a flat slab of stone to observe it more closely.

"This is no ordinary stone. What do you see?"

I accepted the heavy and dark dripping lump and before I could make my own observations Mr Shorto demonstrated the cause of his interest.

"See how it is formed. It has the appearance of once being a liquid for the flow is curiously preserved. Henry Chalk, it is now my turn to surprise you."

I could see by the excited expression upon the face of my companion that he was indeed certain of the origins of this piece and I urged him to inform me of the nature of his discovery.

"Iron has been made upon this very spot. This piece is the waste residue perhaps from the early manufacture of iron."

I looked about at the quiet meadow for it appeared a world away from dark industry and ironworking but before I could question Mr Shorto further he raised himself and urged me to follow.

"Come. Somewhere close at hand we shall find iron ore for you cannot make iron without it."

With the commencement of our search for iron ore I now embraced this most welcome distraction for it drew our attention to the ground beneath our feet and away from the conspicuous edifice that was the creation of the Caliph of Fonthill, Mr William Beckford.

Amongst the stubble in nearby fields we soon encountered further pieces of the dark grey residue from

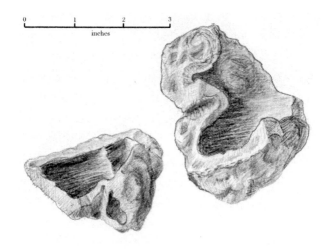

Tisbury Iron Ore

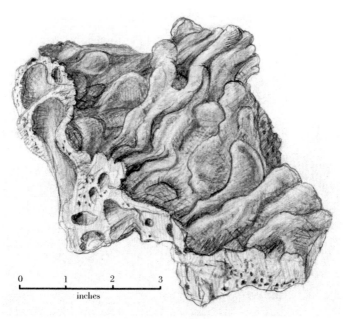

Tisbury Slag

the iron making process but also the heavy crimson and rust brown pieces of iron rich stone from which iron is formed and we began gathering it up as if there were indeed some purpose to this action. In time we rested upon a large bank in the shade of a mighty oak tree to view the haul of stones at our feet.

"Well, I have been in your company not two whole days and I am now a fervent collector of stones. It is a consequence of being abroad with Henry Chalk."

I questioned my companion on what was to be done with this heap of heavy stones and Mr Shorto feigned his surprise;

"Why to make iron of course for South Wiltshire iron must be a rare commodity indeed. I will one day return to collect our pile and I shall know where to find it, for our old friend here shall not be moving far."

Mr Shorto slapped his hand upon the rugged bark of the great oak tree beside us.

"In truth Henry I do not understand the process of iron making that was employed here. I have witnessed upon my excursion to Ironbridge the same early residue for it is found in places where iron is produced today. Indeed this "cinder" or "slag" as it is termed can be introduced to the blast furnace for it still contains a good proportion of iron. Is it not heavy in the hand?"

There ensued some speculation upon the birth of iron making and Mr Shorto adjudged that iron ore would be combined with charcoal and a simple furnace might be constructed to produce a small volume of wrought iron. There must also be a supply of oxygen to increase the temperature of this operation and to this end a pair of bellows should suffice. Here at Tisbury, with the final formation of the iron, the slag has been made to drain from the raging furnace and flow sufficiently so as to form the quick to harden residues that remain for us to find in the stream bed and the soil. The wrought iron bloom is gone from this place for that is prize.

"The making of iron began in a simple way, as must all things Henry. I cannot say whether we have today encountered the cradle of an ancient industry but neither do I see the remnants of the blast furnace."

I stated to Mr Shorto that iron objects were indeed absent from the South Wiltshire barrows and the discovered metal pieces were confined to brass, copper and gold. My friend confirmed that brass is a combination of copper and tin and so some ancient understanding of the transformation and the alloying metals was therefore understood.

"It is curious Henry, with the apparent ubiquity of iron ore in our country, that iron was not the first metal to be produced. I can only surmise that the greater temperatures that are required for the manufacture of iron were beyond the capabilities of these first ancient metalworkers."

We both lapsed into a thoughtful silence and lay back upon the bank to observe the colossal oak tree with its

mighty girth, prospering here in the iron rich soil. If ever
a natural object should possess the wisdom of years then
surely within this majestic tree with its great spread of
trunks and finer branches, heartwood and root there is
a power forged through countless seasons. To sit in its
welcome shadow is to be touched by a presence that is
greater than the objects formed by man's intervention. I
have scaled Silbury Hill and walked amongst the raised
stones of Stonehenge but they do not readily whisper their
purpose. A tree surely has no purpose other than to live
and to promote life about it and yet our reverence is surely
better directed towards a grand and ancient tree rather
than an anciently adjusted stone. I sensed that Mr Shorto
was also reluctant to move from this close affiliation with
nature and his mood was reflective after long and silent
meditation.

"Henry, consider if you will all the iron and steel that
is deemed essential to our existence in the world today
and here at our feet is heaped the earthly fruit that enables
such enterprise. Ancient man once sought the best quality
flint, as you have recently discovered, in the mines behind
the Winterslow Hut and flint was once indispensible. Man
will make progress, for such is our restless nature and so
the following generations have abandoned one stone in
favour of another."

I lamented the passing of the distant flint era and
suggested that there was once a simplicity to the

requirements of ancient man that is now lost to us.

"This was surely once a more brutal world Henry and that is not an attribute that I readily associate with you."

After considering this statement I confessed that as I was unable to deal a fatal blow to a fish for fear of hurting that creature then perhaps Mr Shorto was correct in his judgement.

As the sun dappled through the gently rustling leaves of the giant oak tree Mr Shorto dug deeper into my soul and I could but listen to this pervading wisdom.

"Henry, I have read in your own words how your eminent friend Sir Richard Colt Hoare sought sanctuary in the study of ancient antiquities as a distraction from the grief that he bore from the loss of his dear wife Hester. I adjudge that you are finding a similar distraction in a study of the flint age. The death of your father looms large as does the earlier death of your dear mother and the study of anciently worked flint is a comfortable world away. You are soon to meet with Miss Sarah Foster and it is surely time for the affairs of the heart to come before the commonplace business of the brain. You are young and there is time enough ahead for the study of old things."

I now helped Mr Shorto to his feet and we bid our silent farewells to the ancient tree and set off slowly for the village of Hindon where I first met Miss Sarah Foster in such fortuitous circumstances. The conundrum of the lost era of Tisbury iron must await the arrival of the industrial antiquary to establish a satisfactory resolution but my host and I are in agreement that we have by chance undertaken "A Tour in Search of Iron" and such was our toast at dinner at the Deptford Inn.

I wish you goodnight my dear uncle and trust and hope that weary limbs assist with a swift passage to unhindered sleep for otherwise there is much to keep me tossing and turning in my bed.

Your faithful Nephew
HENRY CHALK.

Saturday 10th September 1808

MY DEAR UNCLE,

I have indeed slept better than I expected and at breakfast
I sent a note to the George Inn in the High Street, advising
Mr Robert Foster of my address in Salisbury. Within the
hour Robert Foster was standing before me and I could
not take the smile from my face as I introduced Robert to
Mr Shorto. There is so much that I need to convey to my
good friend and not least the discovery of the publication
of my private correspondence but all must wait until there
is time enough to do so. My host suggested that it was akin
to the meeting of two brothers such is the familiarity that
exists between Robert and myself and he confessed that it
has warmed his heart to witness such friendship. Robert
has assured me that his sister has promised not to stray
from their accommodation whilst he is absent for you will
no doubt recall that it was just such a circumstance that
caused the meeting between Miss Sarah Foster and myself
in the first place.

"Mr Shorto, you will know by now that whither Mr
Chalk goes then disruption shall soon follow."

My host stated that we had last evening returned safely

from a short pedestrian tour and the acquiring of blisters upon his feet was the only mishap to befall us so perhaps their mutual friend was changing his ways.

"Sir, let us hope so. Henry, to avoid any confusion on the matter, please will you confirm that you are to meet with Sarah and myself at 3 o'clock within the Northern Porch of Salisbury Cathedral?"

My heart gave a giant leap upon hearing these words and I swiftly gave Robert my firm acknowledgement that this was indeed my intention and he checked his watch by Mr Shorto's longcase clock who confirmed the accuracy of this magnificent timepiece.

Our visitor now appeared impatient to depart and displayed not the usual ebullience that I associated with my friend. I now asked for Robert's assurance that all was as it should be and after a pause he admitted to an unsettling circumstance that had not long occurred upon leaving the George Inn to find his way to Rollestone Street.

"Henry, you will recall at the Winterslow Hut where across the hallway from your door lay the ailing doctor who on the night of the great storm stole a horse and saddle and then vanished into the night?"

I stated that despite the blow to my head I could remember clearly this circumstance although I never encountered the man who purported to be a doctor. I added that a number of other private possessions had gone missing and their loss was attributed to this same man.

"Well, whilst his door was open I did enter his room to ensure that all was well as I thought his illness genuine and although he soon waved me away there was sufficient light to see his features clearly enough. I am blessed Mr Shorto for once I have seen a face I never forget it and today, Henry, on my way here, I have just passed by this same man in the streets of Salisbury. It took a further twenty or more paces for me to recall where I had before encountered this man and I then turned about to seek out this thief in the crowded street. To my surprise I found that this man had already paused at the corner to observe me and as a consequence of my looking back our eyes met for the briefest of moments. In a flash he was gone and I hastened to retrace my steps but upon rounding the corner and amongst the busy street I could find no trace of this rogue for he was quick to step into an alley or a shop doorway to avoid my interest. Henry, I do not believe that he is at all a good man for I witnessed malevolence in those staring eyes.

Please forgive and excuse me gentlemen for I am perhaps overly anxious on this day and it is all the fault of Mr Henry Chalk. I promised Sarah that I would not linger for she knows well enough my propensity for chatter so a messenger I must be. We shall meet again Mr Shorto. Henry, I look forward to the appointed hour."

Mr Shorto suggested that he would now escort Robert Foster back to the George Inn to ensure that all was well with a curious request that in his short absence I should not stray from the house. I am left to wonder at the identity of the ailing doctor and the wrong doings he may now be embarked upon in Salisbury.

I still await Mr Shorto's return but I have nothing more to add for I shall only confess to my fretful condition before the time has come to again meet with Miss Sarah Foster.

After this day my dear uncle it is my intention to return to Southwark where I shall make all the necessary arrangements for you to soon join me at Chalk's Brewery as my partner in business.

Your devoted Nephew,
HENRY CHALK.

*Correspondence to Mr Richard Fenton of Glynamel,
Fishguard, Pembrokeshire.*

Wednesday 24th May 1809

MY DEAR MR FENTON,

I thank you Sir for your kind and sympathetic correspondence and now humbly apologise for my lengthy silence. Indeed it is Miss Foster herself who has encouraged me to be receptive to your appeal to again take up my pen after all these months and I draw upon her strength and support to steady my hand. I must learn from the course of my father's life and I shall not enter that cold and dark place called despair and by the recording of that fateful day and the ensuing turmoil I may yet begin to purge a great evil from my life.

My dear friend I must not procrastinate further and I now cast my mind back to the events of 10th September of last year and return in my thoughts to Mr Henry Shorto's house in Rollestone Street where I am in a condition of great excitement for I am soon to meet with Miss Sarah Foster and her brother Robert at the northern porch entrance to Salisbury Cathedral. If I were a magician I should alter the events upon that dread day and report instead that we drank tea at the George Inn for the duration of the afternoon or even examined with interest the silver gravy boats in Mr Shorto's shop in Queen's Street. It was not to be.

Mr Shorto assured me over and again of the accuracy of his longcase clock and also that he should soon be required to replace his worn floorboards after my incessant pacing up and down.

"Henry let us instead wear out the footways in the City if you are to continue in this manner. My family are not yet due to return and so, if you are agreeable, I shall accompany you and we may occupy ourselves until the time of your meeting."

I readily accepted Mr Shorto's suggestion and without explanation we left not by the front door but instead by the rear entrance of his house. I followed my host through the confined Three Cups Chequers to emerge into Winchester Street where we met with the outgoing tide of the gradually disbanding Saturday market. Small driven herds and gaggles of livestock and birds together with pedestrians and carts were now departing from their chaotic congregation in the market place and we crossed between a number of these straggling processions to make our way to St Ann's Street. Hats and eyebrows were raised upon the occasion of the esteemed cutler Mr Henry Shorto treading with care along the back lanes of the City. My companion stated that it was his intention to visit St Martin's Church but Salisbury Cathedral now loomed majestically in the opposing direction and I confessed to being helplessly drawn to the appointed meeting place despite there being a good hour at our disposal. Mr Shorto soon acquiesced but stated that if I had no objection he would accompany me until the arrival of Robert and Sarah Foster. Forgetting that my private affairs had been scattered about the bookstands like washing left out to dry upon the hedgerows I stated with some reticence that Miss Foster had been made sightless from an early age and I wished to inform my friend of this fact before introductions were made. Mr Shorto gripped my arm and halted before addressing me earnestly.

"My dear Henry, I have spent a restless night considering this circumstance after reading again the account of your first meeting with Miss Foster in Hindon. Love shall overcome such obstacles and you know this to be true with all your heart. Indeed if any uncertainty exists then Miss Foster shall soon dispense with it and I shall eat your snakecatcher's hat if I am to be proved wrong."

I could only smile at the return of my oft repeated pledge and thanked my good friend for his concern but stated plainly that I harboured no such doubts.

Upon entering the Cathedral Close through St Ann's gate Mr Shorto could now barely contain himself at the prospect of my meeting again with Miss Sarah Foster and was irrepressible in his chatter and he recommended many interesting features within the Cathedral that we should seek out including the tomb of D'Aubigny Turbeville who was once a great oculist of this City. I was not required to ask after the deeds of this eminent gentleman for the plight of the unseeing world was now perhaps at the forefront of my friend's thoughts and I was hastily supplied with every detail and learnt that his most effective treatment was to extract iron splinters from the eye with the aid of a lodestone. The afflicted came from far and wide and from such remote quarters as the West Indies in search of the services of D'Aubigny Turbeville and it was once common to witness visitors in the streets of Salisbury with green silk over their faces or one or more eyes bandaged.

My friend then looked aghast and hastily apologised for his tactlessness in referring to such matters for he did not wish to cause offence.

"I am sorry Henry for I believe that I am nervous and am talking for the sake of talking so please forgive me."

We turned a corner and Salisbury Cathedral was soon revealed, rising from its spacious grass surrounds with the sporadic elm trees dwarfed by this breathtaking fulfilment of medieval vision. My heart dropped to my boots at this sight and I now believed that I had made a gross error for how could words alone convey to Miss Sarah Foster the awe experienced by the viewer or indeed the scale of such endevour. Upon reaching the Northern porch Mr Shorto insisted that we tucked ourselves inside and did not loiter in plain view although in my distracted silence I cared little where I was positioned and so did not question this action. I now realise that this clandestine behaviour in concealing ourselves from view and by earlier leaving Mr Shorto's house by the servant's entrance was brought about by a degree of caution as to the presence in Salisbury of the mysterious ailing doctor whose sighting in the morning by Robert Foster had caused some concern amongst my good friends. Indeed it was kept from my ears at the time that this rogue upon meeting Robert Foster's gaze in the street, did draw his finger across his own throat in a most threatening manner before disappearing from view. Robert was unsettled by this action and did caution Mr Shorto to be on his guard also.

In the Northern porch my racing mind was now directed to other matters and I welcomed the distraction of a small wandering dog as it entering this roomy antechamber which provides the main public entrance to Salisbury Cathedral. This scruffy four legged visitor soon cocked its leg and then appeared to enjoy the sound of his own voice enlarged inside this high stone porch and barked once more before leaving with an air of satisfaction and renewed importance.

A man with a crooked back and an ancient long grey wig then stumbled over the departing dog and uttered an unholy curse before taking a swipe at the animal with what appeared to be a hazel stick. The dog easily evaded the swinging blow and the irascible fellow continued towards the door of the main building muttering to himself and tapping furiously at the flag stones with his stick. By the opening and closing of this internal door there was released briefly into the porch the ethereal voice of a lone chorister amplified by the vastness within and it is a sound surely intended to transport even the most casual of visitors to believe that they are in the presence of angels. With the door closed I could now barely detect the heavenly voice and yet I was struck by the drifting notes of the chorister and indeed even by the short echoes of the barking dog from a moment before for are these not sounds enhanced by the fabric of the building and its architecture? More visitors to Salisbury Cathedral came and went and Mr Shorto was required to smile politely and bid good afternoon to the respectable natives of Salisbury but refrained from explaining as to why he should be standing in the shadows of the Northern porch. He consulted his fob watch and stated quietly that there was still three quarters of an hour until Miss Foster and her brother Robert were due to arrive and that his jaw now ached from having to smile at every passing acquaintance. To the long suffering Mr Shorto's consternation I suddenly announced that I now intended to dash to the City to make an important purchase thereby causing him to plead in whispered exasperation to explain myself. My friend appeared blank faced as I described the occurrence of a sudden epiphany by my listening to the amplified sounds of this cavernous stone building.

"Henry I do not readily understand the connection between choristers and barking dogs and what is it that you need to purchase in such a rush? I beg that you pause .. and then take a breath before commencing for you shall only confuse me further. Good afternoon ..Mr and Mrs Gosling."

I did as instructed and gathered my thoughts;

"You have informed me that you have read again the account of the circumstances of my meeting with Miss Sarah Foster. Do you not agree that we conducted ourselves upon equal terms until daybreak informed of Sarah's condition?"

My friend nodded in agreement and then smiled wearily;

"Mr Bye.. it is indeed a fine afternoon.. Henry this is intolerable, pray continue."

"I believe that you thought me not listening when you described how those visitors to Salisbury seeking the treatment of D'Aubigny Turbeville wore green silk to cover their eyes? Without realising it you have provided the solution to my dilemma for although I have no such affliction I shall now wear my own blindfold so that I may depend upon the remaining senses whilst we enter Salisbury Cathedral. Every soul who visits this place is humbled by the scale of this edifice and it is through both the eyes and the ears that this shall occur. Neither Miss Foster or I have before set foot inside Salisbury Cathedral and so there may yet be a condition of equality upon our visit but I must delay no longer if I am to execute this plan."

Mr Shorto was now in a further quandary for he did not wish me to be at large upon the streets of Salisbury and by his expression he questioned the sense of my proposal whilst I also wondered whether Miss Foster would herself ridicule this contrivance.

"No, I shall go Henry and you must stay here and do not move from this spot. I have just time enough to dash to Rollestone street and return before the appointed hour. Mrs Shorto has a collection of silk scarves. Pray do not move."

I thanked my friend for his understanding and he now departed briskly, perhaps with some relief that he was no longer required to greet each Salisbury resident as they passed through the Northern porch.

I now realised that my boots had collected a deal of mess from walking the back lanes of Salisbury amongst the market traffic and so I used the iron boot scraper at the entrance to the porch to remove this unpleasantness before I was to soon enter the Cathedral. It was necessary to support myself upon the smooth marble pillars of the stone archway whilst scraping the sole and heal of each boot and as I did so I felt a bump from behind. I turned to find the irascible gentleman with the ancient grey wig who in passing from the building had paid no heed to my presence and uttered a curse upon encountering me in his way. I hastily apologised but the crooked man continued on his muttering course prodding his stick before him and with head down he proceeded to turn the corner to the west of the building.

Having cleaned my boots I dutifully returned to my position to wait and hope that brother and sister would not think me a complete fool and in nervous preparation I now closed my eyes. With my hands concealed behind my back I let my fingers explore the cold texture of the stonework whilst I listened to the ingress and egress of visitors to Salisbury Cathedral.

My dear Mr Fenton, I have never before disclosed the circumstances of Sarah's blindness and she herself remembers but little of the severe fever that struck on the occasion of her fifth birthday. Robert has informed me that he recalls the dark room in which his younger sister lay when even the smallest inundation of daylight caused distress and pain to the feverish child. Mr and Mrs Foster were unremitting in their bedside vigil and in time the fever abated with their daughter joyfully reclaimed from those deathly regions. That any intruding daylight no longer caused distress to the severely weakened child was at first considered a symptom of her recovery but Sarah was unable to gaze upon the anxious faces at her bedside. With the return of the visiting Medic he proclaimed the patient to be blinded by the fever and so the young girl had now emerged into a world of darkness. The family did not give up hope that Sarah's eyesight would soon return and as she grew stronger every treatment was sought and applied. In the following weeks and months Mr and Mrs Foster saw their young daughter suffer the leeches, cupping and a variety of mercurial remedies until they eschewed all such treatment as causing sickness and undue distress. Sarah herself wished not to be cosseted but instead displayed a wilful determination to find her way in a sightless world often to the alarm of her parents with the many bruises of her venturing forth evident for all to see.

Sarah's plight has indeed directed the course of her elder brother's life as he has thrown his wholehearted support into the very recent formation of the West of England Eye Infirmary in the City of Exeter where he will very soon study under the oculist William Adams. Robert hopes that it will become a most progressive institution and that new research shall one day alleviate his younger sister's condition. For some considerable time Robert did not disclose the purpose of his restless travel to every hospital and specialist up and down the Country and to Edinburgh also to establish the best science that may be applied to assist with the recovery of Sarah's eyesight. Miss Sarah Foster is, however, as sharp as a pin in her understanding and did permit her brother to believe that she knew not of his tireless pursuit but now all is discussed openly for the events of this day have caused our world to be turned upon its head.

By the time of Mr Shorto's return my eyes had long since reopened with my thoughts racing hither and thither and I now entertained grave doubts as to my intended course and had all but abandoned the notion of applying a blindfold at all. My companion announced that Robert and Sarah Foster awaited me outside upon the lawn for he had accompanied them from the High Street. Rather than rush to Rollestone Street he had instead purchased a green silk scarf from a haberdashers and also a length of silk ribbon that may assist in binding ourselves in some way as we conducted the tour. I thanked Mr Shorto for his consideration and that I would later reimburse him for the cost of these purchases whilst I thought that I might now conceal them in my pocket and make no reference to Robert and Sarah of my earlier notion. My friend now bit his lip in consternation.

"My dear Henry, upon leaving the haberdashers with the silks in my hand I near collided with Robert and Sarah in the High Street. Introductions were made..and indeed Miss Foster is very beautiful and it did quite disarm me. I explained that I was fulfilling an errand for you Henry and when Robert suggested that if these silks were not a gift for his sister then perhaps they were intended for another admirer.. I found myself reddening at this good natured flippancy .. and so I uttered the truth for I knew not what else to say and I make a very poor liar. Upon hearing my explanation Miss Foster laughed and said; "Trust Henry Chalk to think of such a thing". Robert then stated that they were very early in making their way to the Cathedral as Sarah had grown impatient of waiting at the George Inn and at this disclosure he was scolded by his sister for always talking too much."

Mr Shorto now appeared quite forlorn as he explained these circumstances as if he were in some way at fault.

"Henry, before I depart to soon welcome my own family on their return to Salisbury I must inform you that Miss Foster has since requested that if it is indeed your intention to apply the silk scarf then it should be done before you are to meet. I will assist if you wish. I believe that Sarah fully respects your desire to restore the equality that existed at your first meeting and I do not think that she will mock you at all."

With this reassurance I folded the green silk scarf over and over and placed it before my eyes and turned about to enable Mr Shorto to tie it tightly from behind. He then pressed the length of silk ribbon into the palm of my hand and I thanked him warmly for being a true friend.

"I will be thinking of you Henry and good luck. I shall ask Robert and Sarah to enter the porch so that you may now conduct your tour. I would still advise caution when you are at large upon the streets of Salisbury and do not walk alone lest the ailing Doctor is still lurking and as neither you nor I know his face then be careful of any that approach you."

I could hear Mr Shorto's departing footsteps and as I strained to listen to other movement within the porch it was my own short and rapid breathing that filled my ears. The first voice in the darkness was that of Robert Foster.

"Well Henry in true fashion you have indeed done the strangest thing. Sarah is here beside me."

"Good afternoon Henry, so shall it be the blind leading the blind?"

To hear Sarah's voice again, after the passing of almost an entire year, caused my mouth to become dry and my whole body to quiver with excitement and anxiety in equal measure. So much has been written with Robert the conduit for all that has passed between us but nothing shall supplant hearing again the voice of one who has occupied my thoughts night and day since the time of our encounter in Hindon. There was indeed no apprehension in Sarah's voice and for all the world I wished to tear the silk from my eyes and look again upon her face but her good humour and understanding did embolden me to have faith in my contrived sightlessness.

I shall try also to document my own words so that there shall be a parity of dialogue to make some sense of our encounter.

"Good afternoon Sarah I am so very pleased that you have come but I dare not move from this spot without guidance. Mr Shorto has purchased a length of ribbon that may assist.."

"Then I shall take Robert's arm and we may both hold the ribbon and in this way proceed together."

With her brother placing one end of the ribbon in his sister's hand I gripped the opposing end firmly as if my life depended upon it.

The lone chorister's voice had now ceased by the time that we entered the main building and I felt a sudden vulnerability as we progressed slowly in our curious triumvirate. The close comforting references were our own footfalls or a swish of clothing but beyond there existed in the darkness only a soft cacophony of blurred disturbance. To be denied the sounds of middle distance ensures that no plan or map may be formed in the mind and all is therefore confusion. For the sightless I now believed it to be a place of intimidation and this cavernous building even reduced the English voices of the shuffling tourists to a conspiratorial Babel where I could not discern one familiar word and I wondered what I had caused Sarah to endure by my suggestion.

Robert soon assuaged my discomfort as he informed us that we were now at the Western end of the Cathedral and before us stood a succession of great columns linked by fine pointed arches and these flanked the broad and empty nave. Further tiers of columns and arches soared heavenward and below the distant vaulted ceiling harmonious lines of long clear glass windows cast down a flood of white light to illuminate this main body of the Cathedral. An elegance of gothic design and repetition could now be imagined but I held a picture of the exterior of this extraordinary structure in my mind and so my task was made all the easier. For Sarah's benefit her brother suggested that he described the form of the Gothic arch upon the back of her hand with his finger to which she consented. After Robert's subtle demonstration of such gargantuan load bearing design upon his sister's skin and her laugh as he confessed to being no draughtsman I was tugged into motion by the silk ribbon.

"Keep up Henry or we shall leave you behind."

Sarah's voice caused me to forget my concerns and I wrapped the ribbon around and around my finger bringing me ever closer to Sarah so that her scent now enveloped my senses and any mustiness of this building or the tobacco ridden odours of passing tourists were now expunged by her close proximity. Sarah had indeed reciprocated in keeping the silk ribbon taut between ourselves and I gauged that she too had twisted it tight around her own finger. The tightness of the silk ribbon caused my finger to throb but to feel the presence upon the opposing end of our attachment was all that concerned me and my heart soared ever higher with each transmitted motion.

Robert now described how there were tombs positioned along the length of the nave between the great stone columns and some of these carved recumbent statues were perhaps the early Bishop's of Salisbury. I was content to pass by these stone figures and continue on our sedate procession for all eternity but Sarah was drawn by Robert's comment that one subject had suffered greatly at the hands of the tourists for the tomb displayed an array of graffiti. Sarah expressed a desire to examine it for herself if such a thing was permitted and her brother considered that there should be no objection as long as she did not intend to contribute to this disfiguration. He added that neither did there appear to be any officer of the church in sight to request such permission. Our guide explained that these tombs were positioned upon a plinth that first must be negotiated.

"Then assist dear brother and show Henry also where he must step."

Robert guided Sarah and myself to climb up a full step to reach the tomb and once elevated we positioned ourselves on either side of the recumbent figure with the ribbon falling slack between us.

"Thank you Robert."

It was as if this were a signal for our chaperone to remove himself from our immediate company whilst we explored with our fingers the effigy of the long dead gentleman who lay before us.

"I shall now examine the choir stalls," announced Robert taking empathetic note of his sister's wishes but he added that we should not move from this plinth for the flag stones below would be most unforgiving.

As Robert departed I heard a brisk tapping upon these same flagstones accompanied by an incomprehensible muttering and I judged this to be the same irascible gentleman in the ancient grey wig passing close by and I afforded myself some silent reassurance by this unsighted recognition.

"Our figure is much worn Henry. His fingertips have crumbled and many visitors have inscribed their names upon him."

I explained that the carving was made easily into a soft stone and it was perhaps alabaster. I could judge by her response that Sarah was smiling.

"Trust you to have a word on the stone. And what stone would you wish to be carved from when you are gone, it should perhaps be chalk?"

I laughed at this whispered suggestion in the darkness and listened to my response as if it were another's voice and not my own.

"Then my features would wear all too quickly. Sarcen stone would tax the sculptor and all but the most persevering tourist would not scratch their name upon me. I do not like to think of when I am gone from this world for I believe that my life is just begun."

As we roved the cold and smooth effigy before us our finger tips brushed together and we both gasped at this contact. Of a sudden the cathedral clock commanded three

resounding chimes from some unchartable position above
our heads and I waited for these great bells to cease their
hum whilst I gathered my thoughts.

"Sarah, you will recall in the carriage once the dawn
had intruded upon our special journey when you read my
features with your tender touch? I shall not, for as long as
I live, forget that moment."

My fingers explored the nose and mouth of the supine
figure before me in vain hope that I might again encounter
warm skin rather than cold alabaster.

"Have I spoken out of turn my dearest Sarah? Or
reminded you of something that you wished to forget?"

I could not bear this close silence and I believed
that Sarah had been offended by my blundering in the
darkness. With my heart racing I slowly lowered my arm
to make the ribbon taut once more so I might again locate
Sarah's reassuring presence but the ribbon was weightless
and unattached and I hastily gathered the full length of
silk between my cupped hands. As if I were drowning in
an unseeing world, I pulled down my blindfold and found
myself alone upon the plinth.

My dear Mr Fenton I cannot truly recall the order of
my panic at the realisation that Sarah was no longer before
me and connected by our length of silk ribbon. With
the freedom of sight all was incomprehensible and my
eyes struggled against an assault of daylight and gothic
grandeur amidst which I only wished to locate Sarah and

restore the calm intimacy of our meeting. I did not call out
her name for this was surely a game of hide and seek or a
trick played out upon the unsuspecting Henry Chalk with
Robert an accomplice to this charade and both would soon
reveal themselves. Even the tourists had receded to the
extremities of the Cathedral and I was left alone, turning
in circles, at the very centre of the building beneath the
great tower and spire. I looked in turn behind the choir
screen but found no persons there and ran also the length
of the nave before passing through the Northern porch and
outside to the open lawns but of brother and sister I could
find no trace. I told myself to return to where I last heard
Sarah's voice and I inspected all around the figure of Sir
John Cheney but to no avail and I soon found myself again
standing directly beneath the spire not knowing what to do.

A small pale object caught my eye as it drifted slowly
through the air to rest upon the stone floor of the spacious
Northern Transept. I took the thirty or more paces from
my central position to retrieve and examine this curiosity
and found it to be a once white handkerchief but now worn
and discoloured and spotted with fresh blood. My instinct
was to hastily discard this soiled handkerchief but it must
have fallen from somewhere and so it was that by raising
my gaze I saw Miss Sarah Foster standing stock still upon
the very edge of an upper tier of the higher reaches of this
building.

I cried out as soon as I could gather enough air into my

lungs;

"Sarah, do not move one inch forward. Please oh please
be as still as you can. I am coming for you."

By the time my words skewed to all lofty corners of the
Cathedral's interior I was already in flight to seek a means
by which to gain access to these upper levels. In the far
corner of the Northern Transept I found an open door to
a spiral staircase and I bound up these tightly arranged
worn stone steps with only an infrequent narrow window
by which to find my footing. I stumbled many times and
rasped my shins against stone whilst my arms thrashed at
the walls to haul me ever higher. I could not comprehend
why Sarah would have wandered so or found her way to this
most precarious position and I hoped in desperation that
she would heed my words and not move even a fraction of
an inch. Into the light I emerged and my eyes sought and
found with relief the blessed figure of Sarah standing upon
the ledge with a great void between us and the open floor
of the Northern Transept far below. I dashed before the
extraordinary stained glass windows with their many bright
colours flickering in my vision and once upon the same
side of the upper transept I slowed to a walk and confirmed
my intention to come to her. Still she did not move and I
reached out to take her hand talking all the while though
I know not what words passed my lips. As she gripped my
fingers tears of joy rolled down my cheeks in celebration of
a tragedy averted but rather than withdraw from the edge

Sarah stated quietly and calmly.

"Henry, we are not alone."

I could not comprehend these words nor the fact that Sarah was immovable from her position with the tip of her shoes protruding out into thin air. I turned about and from the shadows a figure advanced slowly towards us across this broad upper floor whilst I peered to see who this might be that was inexplicably the cause of Sarah's immediate peril. The face that slowly emerged was a distant memory ravaged by time and when he spoke his voice was known to me and a paralysis gripped my body.

"You appear worried my dear nephew, well I suppose you have good cause."

The man halted behind Sarah and I listened to the disbelief in my tremulous voice.

"Uncle James, is it you?"

"It is indeed your dear uncle, or the "ailing Doctor" you may call me what you will."

Without turning about Sarah took a deep breath before asking in a whisper after her brother.

"He is ..resting.. in the choir stalls, troublesome fellow that he is. He shall not I fear witness the tragedy of an impossible love when two lovers leap to their deaths bound by a pledge of eternal love and a silk ribbon. Henry you really have made my task all the simpler. It shall be clear to any that try to resolve this.. tragedy that the lovers wished their chaperone to be indisposed whilst they make their leap to find peace and equality in another world. Well that is how I view it. I shall take good care of Chalk's Brewery for I am the sole remaining eligible relation, as you well know. Think on it as a moment of liberation, you no longer have to write your interminable letters and I no longer have to read them whilst I plot your demise. Now, I shall not detain you. Henry you have the silk ribbon still in your clutches and I shall thank you for the return of my handkerchief. We could not wait here all afternoon my dear nephew for you to find us and so my handkerchief drew your attention as I knew it would. You will note that the little vixen drew my blood whilst we made our acquaintance. Henry stop shaking and pull yourself together. Tie the ribbon to Miss Foster's wrist and then attach it to your own."

In this nightmare I was compliant to my uncle's every instruction for he only had to press his hand into Sarah's back to send her to her death upon the flagstones below.

"Kneeling down would be best, Henry help the lady, have you forgotten your manners? Now pull your blindfold back into position. There are tourists wandering below, let us hope that none look up just yet. You may say your farewells."

As I write these words the sickness that I felt in the pit of my stomach now returns but I shall take a sip of brandy to continue. My uncle's voice haunts me and there is barely a night that passes where I do not awake in a sweat before seeking the reassurance of my flint heart on its chain that I wear always around my neck.

As we knelt side by side upon the ledge, bound by our silk ribbon, neither did Sarah or I utter one word and the silence was broken by a bird as it landed in a fluster beside us.

"Shoo, be off, a wretched pigeon in the house of God. Flight is a most enviable ability, do you not agree? It is however wasted on such creatures."

Assisted presumably by my uncle's boot the pigeon clapped its wings together and departed noisily into the wide open space before us.

"I almost forgot Henry, your mother's ring? Sadly it shall never encircle the finger of your beloved. You may keep the silver clad flint hearts for I am fair sick of flint my dear nephew. You kindly informed me when you left Southwark that you took the ring from the heart shaped box upon your father's desk. Dear, dear Hannah, kept in that dull house with her dull husband, my prissy brother good riddance to him. It is perhaps in your fob pocket?"

The fingers of my right hand went to my fob pocket and inside I felt not a ring but instead a quantity of fine powder. It was indeed loose soil and the minute gold pins from Bush Barrow that the younger Mr Parker had directed towards my boots and I later retrieved to keep for examination. I gathered as much of this fine mixture as I could until I had a small heap within my palm.

"Henry, the ring? Hurry boy."

I mumbled that I could not at first readily pick it out of my narrow pocket. Holding my clenched palm down low I gauged that to retrieve the ring this diabolic fiend would now reach over me to prise the gold ring from my grasp. In my head I counted to three before casting the handful of soil and minute gold pins upwards and backwards and by the exclamation of distress and surprise that followed I knew that I had hit my target.

In this same instant I shouted to Sarah to draw backwards and it was as if she were reading my thoughts for I felt the silk ribbon that connected us tug in one motion. I ripped the blindfold from my face and with panic in my fingers I unravelled the ribbon from my wrist before charging at this demon as he clawed at his eyes to clear the fine dusty soil and minute gold pins. I forced him back against a pillar and smelled the rotten expelled air from his lungs as he gasped into my face. His red and watering eyes half opened and he regained his stance before pushing me backwards towards the edge. He now drew a razor from his pocket and flipped open its blade as he advanced towards me. At my back was the precipitous fall into the Northern Transept and whilst Sarah cried out for help there was no place for me to go but towards the slashing blade.

Behind the dread figure of my villainous uncle, to my great surprise and relief, another person now occupied our ledge and it was the irascible gentleman with the ancient long grey wig who, of a sudden, appeared with stick raised.

He brought down his hazel stick across the back of the head of the advancing d-v-l causing him to crumple momentarily and drop the razor to the floor which in turn skidded across the ledge to clatter down upon the flag stones below.

My uncle James now turned upon the irascible fellow and dealt him a blow to remove the ancient grey wig before gripping him by the throat.

I cried out in amazement at the revealed sight of John Fenton who had all this while been present in the Cathedral.

"John, it is you. How..?"

"Never mind ..that Henry... get this ..murderous.. fiend ...from my.. throat."

Before I could move to assist John Fenton he was cast to one side whilst my uncle made his escape ducking around a pillar and disappearing with his footsteps resounding behind him.

I rushed first to Sarah and she gripped my hands whilst assuring me that she was unharmed but feared desperately for her brother's life. In this same instant John Fenton proclaimed that he could see Robert walking with some uncertainty across the floor below our position. This was good news indeed but I wasted no time in imploring John to assist Sarah in being reunited with her brother and to keep them both safe until my return. Sarah in turn pleaded with me, as I rushed from her side, to let my uncle go and not to pursue him but I was now blind with rage and knew what my action must be.

My dear Mr Fenton, I can write but little more at the present time and I shall dispatch this full and most painful account to you so that you might read for yourself all that occurred. You may be assured that Robert has made a full recovery from the blow to the head that he received at the hands of my despicable uncle and that Sarah has survived the horror of her abduction by this same fiend. I would not be surprised if both brother and sister and the entire Foster household wished for no further association with this troublesome suitor but that is indeed not the case. The inner strength of Miss Sarah Foster has kept me from madness and despair and the love between us has been made all the stronger as a consequence of this dreadful ordeal. Miss Foster is indeed a remarkable woman and I hope that we shall all meet together before too long but I may not at this stage state the purpose of this celebration.

I wished above all to praise the actions of your son John for he did indeed save the lives of both Sarah and myself by his timely and most surprising intervention. You have assuredly heard his version of events but I consider this full account to be my humble duty to describe his brave and valiant efforts. We parted not on the best of terms outside the Salisbury Court after his successful defence of Thomas Targett and the two men from the charge of deer stealing. Indeed I gave him not the credit that his efforts deserved and I was foolhardy not to heed his request for me to remain at the Inn and I instead crept into the public gallery to witness his clever dissection of my published letters to dismiss them as merely a work of fiction. John then departed for Pembrokeshire but unknown to me before leaving the City he purchased, for your perusal, a copy of both "A Tour in Search of Chalk" and "A Tour in Search of Flint". With nothing better to entertain him in the pauses on his journey he read these books from cover to cover and found to his horror embedded in my words sufficient evidence to establish a most malign intent towards me from my sole remaining relation. There was indeed a grave and growing suspicion as to the character of my uncle James shared between my good friends and I include you Sir to the fore of this number. I have learned subsequently that he had written letters to Sir Richard Colt Hoare and to the trustees of Chalk's Brewery demanding in ever more threatening tones that he be made aware of my whereabouts stating that the responsibility as to my well being was his alone and not that of others who bore no Chalk blood in their veins. At the time I suspected an unspoken concern amongst my friends and I know now that my brazen wanderings brought anguish to those who wished me only to be at large in trusted company. I do not consider for one minute that any knew of the extent of the evil that long fermented in the twisted and rotten heart of my uncle James; He who I wished to invite as my partner at Chalk's Brewery.

John pieced together these known suspicions and they were then confirmed to him in black and white upon the page. Knowing that I supplied my uncle with word of my every move he presumed correctly that I had told this villain of my forthcoming meeting with Sarah at Salisbury Cathedral. If a trap were to be set then there was time enough for this villain to creep from his lair to deal me a final blow and dispose of the obstacle that stood between him and the security of Chalk's Brewery. Of course my own foolish antics by applying a blindfold played into the hands of my murderous uncle to make his task all the easier. I could now be dispatched with my beloved Sarah and lo a pact of self murder would be pronounced by the Coroner. John has informed me of his regret at making himself scarce upon seeing Sarah and myself standing at the tomb for he did not wish to intrude or pry at this most intimate moment and so took instead a turn around the cloisters. As the ancient clock struck three Sarah was forcefully and silently abducted and she has told me that the most unspeakable threats were made if she cried out and did not walk with him in a manner so as not to attract unwanted attention from bystanders in the Cathedral at that moment. That Sarah bit my uncle's finger is no small surprise for she is not a meek person given to easy submission but he did smuggle her away to the higher levels of the building and awaited my arrival. Robert Foster was dealt a violent blow upon the head and was laid out in the choir stalls until he awoke in a very giddy condition but mercifully there has been no lasting damage and he is back to his robust self once again. Whilst Sarah and I were perched high up upon the ledge, your son John searched frantically to all points of the compass within the great building and it was but the noisy flight of the departing pigeon that had settled briefly beside us that caused him to look up and so he saw Sarah and myself kneeling in preparation to fall to the stone floor far below. To his horror he thought he may yet be too late to save us but he did not call out for surprise was still on his side and finding the means by which to reach this level he timed his arrival to perfection. Indeed for the rest of my days I shall be eternally grateful to your eldest son John. He has since described how he found the old wig at an Inn upon his return journey where it had apparently been resting on a peg for the last ten years and the hazel stick was torn from the hedgerow once a plan of disguise had been born. Your mischievous son could not resist his play acting whilst I waited at the Northern porch and rather than reveal his presence to me he enjoyed the role of the irascible gentleman bumping into his quarry and cursing all the while.

I must now put down my pen although I have more to relate to you for I have told you nothing of the pursuit of my wretched uncle during which your son again played his part.

Please extend my best wishes to Mrs Fenton and inform

of John's heroic deeds although I feel certain that he will already have done so himself. I hope to visit you again my dear friend when business at Chalk's brewery permits but I shall correspond further to conclude my tale as soon as I am able. I do not have the fortitude now to write another word for it pains me greatly to relive this nightmare.

Your most humble friend
HENRY CHALK.

Thursday 8th June 1809

MY DEAR MR FENTON,

Thank you for your kind words and also the encouragement for me to now complete my tale. In the two weeks since I dispatched my lengthy tract to you I have received some very special visitors. Two days ago Miss Sarah Foster and her brother Robert arrived to take tea with me and indeed a tour of Chalk's brewery ensued. A pall has hung over the brewery but it has been lifted by the effervescent Robert Foster and by his sister Sarah who has won the hearts of many with her smile and also her genuine curiosity into the business of brewing. Brother and sister were able to sample the very first production of Edward Chalk's Golden Pale Ale for which the hard water from the new well is ideally suited and it shall be exported in bottles that have been manufactured especially. My father once abandoned his notion to produce a bottled stout but I have named this pale ale in his honour and memory for I believe that he would have approved of this endevour.

Sarah was then drawn to visit the dray horses for they were now stabled after the day's exertions and she tied a ribbon upon her favourite but there were treats for all the horses that Sarah met.

It is by her guidance that I have placed some of my own books upon the shelves about the house and also in my father's room. Sarah has informed me that it is now my room and will think of me sitting at my desk when I next write. Indeed she believes it to be a good house and perhaps with this blessing the ghosts will one day rest in peace and be no longer bound to pursue me about the place to the relief of all concerned. Sarah then asked, with a knowing smile, if I were now embarked upon the "steady middle ground through life" that my father would have wished for me or whether I still craved "the peaks and troughs of adventure"? These were indeed familiar words and phrases that I recalled from the book "Robinson Crusoe" and indeed I had quoted the very same myself when corresponding with my uncle on my first pedestrian adventure. I now scowled at Robert who protested that it was his sister's demand that he should read aloud from the two published books of my letters and he was only following instructions. Again my every thought and deed is blown into the air like threshed chaff.

I am due this evening to attend the theatre with Robert and Sarah and I am saddened that they are to return home tomorrow after this brief visit to the capital.

As you know Sir, I am due to meet again with Robert and Sarah in one month's time for you have initiated a visit to Holnicote, which is situated not five miles from Minehead, and is the home of Mr and Mrs Martin Fortesque. I sincerely look forward to meeting again with you Sir and perhaps John also and I have before heard Sir Richard Colt Hoare speak with tenderness of his sister's family and their Estate and so it is with great anticipation that I now wait for these intervening days to pass.

I have been blessed with another visitor and Mr Henry Shorto has departed after taking luncheon at my house. His business caused him to travel to London and he thought it rude not to call and whilst he was about it to also inspect my cutlery. Indeed I was able to repay, in a very small part, Mr Shorto's hospitality for he has spent the night under my roof and in the morning I conducted him upon a tour of Chalk's brewery. He has long been fascinated by the story of the digging of the great well and requested that he be allowed to drop a pebble into the darkness and await the sound of broken water echoing up from the depths. Upon his arrival at my house my friend presented me with a small coloured illustration of a red admiral butterfly that he himself has drawn. I could not keep the tears from my eyes when he revealed this gift and I thanked him wholeheartedly and stated that it would now sit upon my desk and forever remind me of my father. Mr Shorto has also given his encouragement for me to put pen to paper and hopes one day to read all in another volume of Henry Chalk's adventures and in doing so he believes that I shall "remove a great burden from my mind". He has instructed

me to proceed as before and record events in the order that
they occurred and for once I will do what I am told.

I shall now do my best to breath life into a sorry tale and
so I recommence where I left off in our position high above
the Northern Transept in Salisbury Cathedral. It was my
own rage that compelled me to leave Sarah and her brother
Robert in the care of your son John and pursue my uncle
whilst he was hindered by having the soil dust and minute
gold pins from the Bush Barrow excavation cast into his
eyes. Along high passageways and up tight and winding
stone staircases I chased my sole relation whilst I could
hear scampering footsteps ahead of me as ever upwards we
traversed this great gothic maze. At the base of the tower
I encountered the ancient clock whilst the afternoon sun
blazed through the long clear glass windows illuminating a
web of structural ironwork but I had no thought to inspect
such features and hastily returned to the enclosed dark
staircases as I continued my ascent. At the next level I
peered briefly at the giant bells but I was now convinced
that I was gaining upon my quarry and so I soon burst out of
my staircase to where the giant windlass is house directly
beneath the spire itself. Now puffing heavily and wild eyed
I ordered the startled windlass operators to confirm that
a man had just this minute passed this way and to a soul
the three men looked heavenward. The interior of the spire
is a great confusion of ancient timbers crossing back and
forth between the tapering stonework and in the gloom

I could now detect a figure ascending the succession of narrow wooden ladders. I hurled myself upon the rungs of the first long ladder and I was soon bouncing and springing as I reached its centre but I cared not for my own safety. As I climbed ever higher I thought of every element of my uncle's evil, the pieces that your son John had so astutely assembled from my published correspondence. In the village of Hindon, upon the night of the election, across the glowing brazier I met with the evil stare of Joseph Barklay who was a bad man in my uncle's employ and he then pursued me but was deterred by the presence of Mr Beckford's dwarf and his henchmen.

I considered also my nocturnal departure from Stourhead House after the foolish butchery experiment that I was encouraged to conduct upon Sir Richard Colt Hoare's deer by your son John and I then took flight to ensure my return to the Stourhead Inn before midnight. Awaiting me at the gatehouse with his knife at the ready was the murderous Joseph Barklay but he was foiled in his work by my youthful haste and his heart then stopped as he gave chase.

I now dwelt upon the night at the Winterslow Hut when I was drawn to entering the room of the ailing doctor just when my candle had become extinguished and there was a period of grave vulnerability before the arrival of Robert Foster. In the darkness I had paused before the open doorway and there I sensed a time from my youth when my uncle had appeared from a darkened room and my mother could be heard sobbing inside. It is but a distant memory but the house was quiet on that day for it was the event of the great hop market in Southwark which was a very gay and popular occasion. Upon seeing my uncle I had fled to the kitchen and he found me clutching at the apron strings of Mrs West and adopting a pleasant manner he proposed an excursion to the Port of London and we departed soon after. My uncle never again set foot across our threshold and indeed he left me at the front door upon our return from the Port. Neither was my mother's laughter heard again within these walls and I now recall that her golden hair was cut short and remained so until the birth of my dear sister. Soon after, both mother and daughter then passed from this world to leave our house a place of perpetual sadness.

Finally upon the occasion of the great tempest, once Robert had departed from the Winterslow hut, I did foolishly return to the flint pit and laboured in the deluge to reveal the secrets of the ancient miners. As I lay bleeding upon the floor of the pit I thought the vision of my uncle standing above me a trick of the mind but indeed it was he that cast down the extracted flint tools upon my head. It was only by the return of the quick thinking Robert Foster that I was retrieved from my chalky grave with my uncle departed upon a stolen horse for he thought his work done.

To return to the Cathedral spire you may imagine

me, my dear Mr Fenton, leaving daylight far below as I ascended each creaking ladder whilst I was forced to grope before me to find the foot of the next ladder. A curiosity caused me to halt for a moment for a pin prick of light entered the darkness through a minute aperture in the mortar and of a sudden I was aware of my position high up in this jumbled wooden frame and shrouded only by a thin cloak of freestone. Perhaps with no fury in my veins I may have become meek and fearful but the creaking and clattering above me spurred me on and I called out the most vile threats into the constricting darkness. I heard my own voice spit out that I should have no mercy when I got my hands upon him and that I wished him dead and in response I heard a whimpering from above. Of a sudden daylight poured down upon me where a small hatch had been opened and I was able to propel myself ever faster now that I could see my way ahead. My quarry now attempted to climb from this aperture whilst I dashed to grab a trailing leg and then pulled with all my might. I heard a scream as I clawed the figure back inside the spire and I continued pulling until the man's terror was plain to see but I had the greatest shock for it was not my uncle's face.

"You are not my uncle." I now gasped.

The man was speechless and appeared to be awaiting the fate that I had promised.

"I apologise with all my heart Sir for I thought you my murderous uncle and now I find that you are not he."

We both now gulped air for a good minute after our exertions before I introduced myself and established that the man's name was Marchant and with shaking hands he lifted up an object that transpired to be a horn, tied upon a piece of string around his neck.

"I blow's me 'orn see."

The man put the instrument to his lips and gave a faint puff that barely caused a note to emerge. He stammered that for a wager he had climbed the spire and was to blow his horn as proof of his deed to those awaiting below. I now put my own head out of the hatch and was required to rub at my eyes before I could see the sky, the far horizon and the City of Salisbury as if it were comprised only of toy houses and by leaning out as far as I dared I peered down towards the base of the Cathedral. My dear Mr Fenton it was as if I were now Lemuel Gulliver bestriding the diminutive Lilliput and yet for all that there was to feast my eyes upon in this strange land I was drawn instead to observe a minute figure crossing with perceptible haste the green handkerchief of grass far below. In vain hope I bellowed forth my uncle's name but my voice travelled no distance at all from this perch amongst the clouds and I hastily thrust the startled man towards the open hatch.

"Quickly man, blow your horn. Blow as if your life depends upon it."

Mr Marchant now popped his head out into the sky and blew with all his might and blew again and again.

I forced myself alongside the horn blower and sure enough this figure that had not long emerged from the body of the Cathedral now paused briefly to peer up towards our position at the tip of the spire. I looked down helplessly as this one ant, amongst a scattering of stationary ants, now hastily continued on its way and in my heart I felt that my villainous uncle had made good his escape whilst I had pursued the wrong man.

I again apologised to Mr Marchant but reminded him that he had after all fulfilled his wager at which he perked up and produced a small flask of brandy from which I gratefully took a sip before we commenced our descent.

Once I had finally returned to the floor of the Cathedral I found John pacing up and down with Robert sat cradling his head beside the tomb of Sir John Cheney and Sarah, who had been standing with her back to me, now turned before I could announce my arrival. There was a palpable relief at my safe return and an urgent enquiry into the whereabouts of my wretched uncle. Three further persons were also gathered and John explained that the Cathedral Vergers had been alerted by the commotion within the Northern Transept and the Close Constable was summoned once John had described the events of the afternoon. I explained to this gathering that I believed I had witnessed my uncle scurrying from the building as I had looked down from an open hatchway at the top of the spire but I was helpless to act and now he may be anywhere in the City or

beyond. I confirmed to the Church Officials and the Close
Constable that I knew not where in Salisbury my uncle
may have secured a room but that he lived in Exeter and
I gave his address and declared that this was indeed the
extent of the information that I could usefully provide. The
two Vergers and the Constable muttered together whilst I
attended to Robert Foster who assured me that he would
live but stated that he could recall nothing of the blow that
he received for it had been administered from behind and
he awoke in the choir stalls with his face pressed against
a hassock.

The Close Constable stated that he would now speak
with the City Constables to see what may be done outside
the walls of the Cathedral Close and we explained that
we would remove to the George Inn in the High Street so
that Robert Foster might rest and recover from his assault.
Once we were installed in a parlour at the George Inn
Robert was able to properly assess the damage from his
attack and demonstrated that a large egg shaped lump had
appeared upon the side of his head;

"Better a lump on the outside my dear sister, than on
the inside. I shall survive."

John now enquired as to how I had managed to make
an ascent of the Cathedral spire in the fruitless pursuit
of my uncle. With some embarrassment I explained that
like a confused blood hound I had followed the wrong
trail that had caused me to clamber to the very tip of the

spire. I then admitted to terrifying an innocent man who was at the same moment ascending the spire to fulfil a wager and I described how I had cursed and threatened at his heels up each of the ten ladders. John looked on with an incredulous expression on his face as he imagined the scene. I concluded my account by stating that the poor fellow was about to cast himself out of a small hatchway at the very top rather than suffer the appalling litany of punishments that I had pledged to undertake and it was only once I had dragged the poor man back inside the spire by his leg that I realised my gross error. John gave a loud snort of laughter and was soon unable to help himself and such was our sense of relief in being safely gathered together that this outburst quickly spread like an infection to Robert Foster who cradled his sore head whilst squeeking with painful yet uncontrolled laughter.

"John..stop…I implore you …please no…"

Sarah at first admonished her brother for such a display but was soon attempting to stifle her own mirth and I was next to follow for the contagion of laughter can be irresistible and it was after all a ridiculous tale. It was perhaps a good antidote for everything that had just occurred and our nerves were assuredly the better for this most inappropriate behaviour.

In the hiatus that followed, for the gravity of the situation was soon to return, I now composed my apology to all present but especially with Sarah in mind for she had suffered a most terrifying ordeal at the hands of my cruel relation and her abduction had been made all the easier by my own voluntary blindness. Before I was permitted to begin my pathetic address John slapped his hand down flat upon the table causing us all to jump from our chairs;

"Henry you have the address of this fiend. We must reach his lair before he does and I'll wager a guinea to a penny that he will rush there now. His game is up here for he has played his hand and we need to be on the next Post to Exeter."

With this he dashed from the building and returned in a short while with two tickets not aboard the Mail but instead The Mercury.

"We depart at eight and let us hope that we can obtain seats upon the inside."

With this next course of action now decided I stated that I must inform Mr Henry Shorto of the hideous drama within the Cathedral and the true nature of my villainous uncle to whom I had entrusted my every thought and deed whilst abroad upon my pedestrian adventures. It was then by Mr and Mrs Shorto's insistence that Robert and Sarah should stay in Rollestone Street until Robert was fully recovered and fit to travel. This was duly arranged and before John and I departed aboard our coach we enjoyed a good meal in the company of Mr and Mrs Shorto who were indeed appalled at the relating of the events within Salisbury Cathedral.

Mr Shorto insisted that he would take up our cause with the Justices in Salisbury and inform them of our plans and he also suggested that upon our arrival in Exeter we should seek this same assistance for we were now certain that our quarry was a very dangerous and unpredictable man.

So it was that John and I gathered ourselves in order to meet our coach at eight o clock in the evening at the Council House but before departing from Rollestone Street I had taken Sarah to one side to ensure that she was recovered from her ordeal. I was about to state that after the events of this day she must surely question her association with me but I was quietly dissuaded from voicing these uncomfortable thoughts.

"Sssh, I know what you are about to say and I wish for no such thing Henry. We are both stronger than that. I am unharmed and Robert shall have an aching head for a day or two. You have had the greater cause for distress for the one that you once trusted has displayed their evil intent towards you and your very foundations will be shaken by this. If you are to pursue this…your uncle… then do so with care and return safely to me."

I took Sarah's hand and she squeezed it tightly and there was no requirement for us to exchange another word before my departure. I sincerely hoped that Robert would not suffer unduly from his blow to the head but he assured me that he fully expected to be able to return to Minehead shortly and he insisted that I should visit their family home

there once the business in Exeter had been attended to.
Robert, in turn, cautioned me to take the utmost care for
this blackguard appeared capable of the vilest deeds and
he was indeed now a most desperate man and all the more
dangerous for it.

Mr Shorto escorted us to meet the coach and he brought
with him two thick coats in case we were required to
travel on the outside. There was by good fortune one seat
available within the coach for a ticket had been purchased
from Salisbury to Exeter but no traveller had arrived to
lay claim to it and so in the blink of an eye John installed
himself within the coach and closed the door. I thankfully
accepted both of Mr Shorto's coats with a promise to return
them and I clambered up to take my place aboard the roof
of the coach. Before we departed John reopened the door to
call up to me that we would exchange seats at Dorchester
and so I settled down for an uncomfortable night. I bid Mr
Shorto farewell and as the coach lurched forward a thought
occurred that it was perhaps my uncle that had purchased
the unused ticket but at our arrival had shrunk back into
the shadows cursing his luck for he was unable to take his
seat with John and I present. I wished to alert Mr Shorto
of this possibility and so I called back to him to be on his
guard and to make haste back to Rollestone Street without
delay.

"He is still here, I am certain of it. Beware for your own
safety."

My friend looked back unable to hear my words above the clattering of hooves but raised his hat before continuing on his unhurried way. I could do nothing but pray that no further harm be inflicted upon my friends and hoped instead that it was now a race to Exeter that would preoccupy my malevolent relation.

I shall not describe our journey Sir, save to say that Dorchester came and went and with every change of horses I returned to my perch upon the outside of the coach. I can recall looking back to witness the sun breaking free of the horizon into a cloudless sky and we appeared to outrun a fleet of warships upon the English Channel that were becalmed upon their westerly progress by an absence of wind but of the stops and places that we passed I can give little account. In truth I cared not whether I rode inside or outside for I had been made numb by the events that had occurred in Salisbury Cathedral and I shuddered over and again at the thought of Sarah standing upon the ledge high above the Northern Transept. John had travelled to Wales and then straight away returned to Salisbury to save the day in the guise of the irascible old gentleman and so it was by my insistence that he should have some degree of comfort within the coach.

We breakfasted at Bridport and it gave me the opportunity to formally thank your eldest son for his quick thinking, bravery and indeed his friendship. John silently considered my words before suggesting that if I really

was that grateful then perhaps he may have the piece of
untouched gammon that was laying idle upon my plate.
As John concluded both our breakfasts he asked about my
uncle and whether he had always been a rogue and how
could such a man have gained my trust?

I explained that I had no contact with my uncle from the
age of seven but one day a surprise package arrived at the
brewery and contained within was a small volume entitled
"A Pedestrian Tour of North Wales, 1805". Inside there
was a dedication to me from my uncle James Chalk and
also a note with his address in Exeter but he counselled
against speaking to my father about the book or of our
renewed contact. He referred to a "misunderstanding" for
which the blame had been unfairly apportioned upon him
and these were the events and concerns of an adult world
that should not trouble the relationship of an uncle with his
only nephew. As I could not speak easily with my father,
either upon matters of business or in our home, I welcomed
the approach of my uncle and so I began some occasional
correspondence and indeed it was the adventurous spirit
of the book that caused me to set forth upon my own
pedestrian excursions. I admitted that I when I first left
my home in Southwark for South Wiltshire with the scent
of adventure in my nostrils there was no other person that
could be the recipient of my correspondence.

John listened patiently and concluded that my uncle's
motives were clear from the start and that I was just an

obstacle to his achieving ownership of Chalk's brewery.

"Your uncle had a plan Henry but he has been thwarted and let us hope that we find further damning evidence at his quarters and that the rogue shall be quickly apprehended and punished."

On the Sunday afternoon we arrived at our destination and put up at the New London Hotel although John and I were required to share a room. We were informed that the inns in Exeter are frequently overflowing with travellers and so we counted ourselves lucky to find a bed at all. We wasted no time in asking directions to Guinea Street and soon found ourselves in a quarter of the City in which the poorest inhabitants lived and worked. Indeed these same circumstances may be found in any city in England but I had no notion when I dispatched my letters that they would arrive in such a place after their collection from the Exeter Postmaster.

We observed from across this grimy street a small property situated next to the Old Golden Lion ale house that appeared to be a tailor's shop and the sign above the door simply read; "Howson – Tailor". Being Sunday it was closed but we had not the time to wait for Monday morning to arrive and so John crossed the street to knock loudly upon the door. An old face appeared at the window and mouthed an obscenity and the small figure gestured for us to go away. John knocked again and on this occasion the bolt was drawn and the door opened sufficiently to enable a little wizened head to appear and the obscenity was now audibly repeated.

By placing his boot in between the door jamb and the door John prevent its immediate closure but provoked a further stream of curses from the unpleasant little man.

John demanded to know whether a Mr James Chalk resided at this address whereupon the man's eyes narrowed tellingly before he spat in John's face and as John recoiled the door was slammed shut. I offered John my handkerchief to wipe his eyes and guided him back down the narrow street. I suggested that the filthy little man was surely not about to cooperate and so we must return to our lodgings to enquire where we may find a Constable or indeed a Justice of the Peace to give authority for a search of the premises in Guinea Street. We soon established that there was no prospect of speaking with a Justice of the Peace on a Sunday and a Constable was equally elusive and so we soon found ourselves again observing the lowly tailor shop from a stinking alleyway across the street.

"Henry I cannot stand here for a moment longer for I will surely wretch."

I stated that I would offer the old tailor money if it would gain his cooperation and so I now banged on the door and a young man's face leered briefly at the window and I was required to knock again and on this occasion the door opened sufficiently for the face to peer out at us. The young man said nothing and held no expression in his face as I explained that we were seeking Mr James Chalk. I then held up a guinea piece and the simple fellow tried to take it from my hand but I withdrew it before requesting that we be permitted entry and he then may have the money. The man looked crestfallen at the disappearance of the golden coin in my closed palm and he opened the door to reach out further into the street. John now seized the opportunity to push open the door at which the fellow stood tamely to one side but with his mouth open and both hands cupped before him to receive the coin.

"Henry do not waste good money on him for he is a simpleton. Let us do our work before the filthy old man returns as I'll wager that the boy is here on his own for the time being."

I could not now renege on the offer of parting with a guinea and so I dropped it into the young man's cupped hands and he stared at it whilst we left him at the open doorway. The ground floor was indeed a shabby tailor's shop and upon a small shelf at the foot of a narrow stairway John spied a pile of letters addressed to Mr J Chalk, 6B Guinea Street Exeter, Devonshire.

"Henry, I recognise your handwriting. We have the right place."

My most recent letters had evidentially been collected from the Postmaster, perhaps by the simple fellow, in readiness for the return of my uncle and I despaired anew at trusting my every thought and deed to one who had long wished me dead.

John now darted up the steep and worm eaten ladder to the next floor and here evidently was the accommodation of the tailor whilst the young man slept in a cot in the shop and I had never before witnessed such squalor and found it hard to imagine how a life could be conducted in these circumstances. Upon ascending a further ladder we now encountered a locked door and John stated that this was surely the room where my uncle James Chalk now resided. The simple fellow had followed us to the top of the small premises and looked on spinning the gold coin around and around in his fingers as we rattled at the door to no avail. He now stooped down in the passageway and placed his hand in a hole in the rotten wall and extracted a large key and then placed it upon the floor beside us.

John snatched up the key and after fumbling with it in the lock it made a heavy click and as he pushed open the door the simple fellow gave a loud shriek beside us and fled down the ladders and after slamming the front door behind him we could hear his heavy footfalls disappearing down the street. My heart was in my mouth as we entered the place of habitation of my uncle James Chalk and the floorboards groaned loudly under our cautious feet.

A single clouded window permitted only a gloomy light by which to view the room and indeed at first there appeared to be little to see for it was sparsely furnished with only a bed, an old writing desk, a simple chair and a large trunk that proved to be locked. Upon the desk under a shroud of dust a number of books were piled up including my uncle's own "Tour of North Wales, 1805" but also books and earlier tours of this same area. Upon inspection I found passages underlined, scribbled marginalia and even whole pages torn from books and it was apparent that there was nothing original about my uncle's book and that it had indeed been plagiarised from existing sources. The two books of my own published letters gathered dust also beneath a pile of my correspondence and John sneezed loudly at the disturbance of so much dust. In a simple draw I found one of my toy soldiers and I recalled my uncle, upon an early visit to our house lining up these soldiers before I would knock them all down again. At the back of the draw I found three further objects and upon my realisation of their significance I slumped forward upon the creaking chair and I confess that I wretched upon the floor at my feet. Sir, it is with the heaviest of hearts that I now describe the confirmation of how my uncle, to whom I once entrusted my every private thought, has been a wreaker of lives and the cause of great evil. As John looked on I at first picked up my father's fob watch with his initials EHC engraved upon the back. This is the watch that was taken from my father as he expired in the street after falling under the coach off Fleet Street and it could mean only one thing, that my wicked uncle was present at that very moment and was surely the cause of his death. The second object was a

small round wooden box with a tightly fitting lid and within
was a curl of golden hair and this sent my fingers trembling
further for I knew it to be my mother's hair. Beside this
box was a folded card with a broken wax seal and upon
the front was my father's name Edward Chalk and inside a
single fine coiled strand of the same golden hair was sealed
to the page with a small blob of wax. Here was the note
that was delivered on the evening when my father departed
from the house and I was never to see him again for he died
later that night in the street under the wheels of a coach. I
now began to shake in the chair as if a fit had overwhelmed
me for my very worst fears had been confirmed before my
eyes.

John assisted me from that wretched room and we
returned to our lodgings at the New London Hotel where
I flung myself upon the bed in despair and could make
no sound at all as if my uncle's hands were gripping me
firmly about the throat. I awoke still in my clothes and
at first believed that I had experienced the very worst of
nightmares but to quickly dispel this notion John burst
into our room and parted the curtains with a flourish to
admit the early morning sun.

"Henry, I have engaged two Constables to escort us
back to the tailor's shop and I have informed them that it
is a murderer that we wish to apprehend. There must be
no delay."

I leapt from the bed and poured some water from the

jug to splash into my face before following John to meet with the two Constables and we then made haste to Guinea Street and to the tailor's shop beside the tavern. The door was already ajar and the Constable's knocked loudly and also called out for any persons to present themselves. Receiving no reply they now entered the building and John guided them to my uncle's room and this door was also open and it was soon apparent that the large trunk, the books and any remaining clothes had been removed. Of the simple fellow or the tailor there was no sign and the Constable's searched high and low and also roused the landlord of the Old Golden Lion tavern to enquire whether any persons had seen a large trunk being removed but all to no avail. With their fruitless search concluded the Constables shrugged and now excused themselves and so we returned to our lodgings with John lamenting that my devious relation had successfully evaded our attentions.

"It would indeed be a grave injustice if your uncle were not punished for his crimes. I sorely regret that instead of sleeping in a chair I did not last night return to stand vigil in Guinea Street for he was surely close upon our heals had we but realised it. I fear that he has now fled the City and there is no knowing where he might be."

John then expressed his concern that I should succumb to a severe melancholy given the great tragedy that had befallen my family but I was able to reassure him that my thoughts were now directed towards the future.

"There is hope within my heart that a condition of happiness awaits and my mind shall not become sick on his account nor my spirit diminish. He is forever gone from my life."

We ate a good breakfast in silence and after pushing away my plate I confirmed that I must now travel to Minehead where I would visit the home of Mr and Mrs Foster for I had arranged to meet with Robert and his sister Sarah there. I knew not how I should be received by this family for all the trouble that I have caused but go I must. John declared that he would accompany me to Minehead for he could then take a packet ship to Milford Haven where it was but a short distance on to Fishguard.

So it was that we left Exeter behind us and I have told you all I know about my wretched uncle and to this day I know not of his whereabouts. He is indeed a wanted man in Exeter, Salisbury and London but with every passing day I now fear less for the safety of my friends or indeed for myself although, if pressed, I cannot readily explain this circumstance. There is still the mystery of the coded message in my father's hand and I send it to you now for many have tried to unlock its secrets but have failed to do so. It is perhaps essential that it remains a mystery.

Sir, I cannot sufficiently convey the gratitude that I hold for your eldest son John. You will know well enough his penchant for raillery and indeed there have been occasions when I have presented an irresistible target for his amusement but I feel that we have both grown to be men since we first met and I now greatly value his friendship. Perhaps one day I may be able to reciprocate for all that he has done. My dear Mr Fenton you also have been a rock that I have been able to cling to in a stormy sea and I look forward to meeting you again shortly at the home of Mr and Mrs Fortesque in Holnicote. Mr William Cunnington and his family have extended the hand of friendship and I greatly value Mr Cunnington's common sense and the ability to see things afresh and adjudge for himself the significance of each of his antiquarian discoveries. Indeed he explores uncharted territories and I look forward to the publication of his Patron's great work Ancient Wiltshire for within shall be described the invaluable contribution of Mr William Cunnington and his stalwart barrow diggers, Mr Stephen and John Parker and of course their surveyor and draughtsman Mr Philip Crocker. I would also include you Sir as part of this most special assembly for your passion is that of the most committed antiquarian and your presence upon such excursions brings a lightness of heart when the excavation of bones and dust may instead become a dry and sombre occasion. I wish you well with your own literary endeavours; "A Historical Tour of Pembrokeshire" that has required many years of study and travel and also a work of satire; "A Tour in Quest of Genealogy" that John informs me that you have been encouraged to complete by the reading of my own two published volumes. I am indeed flattered but I shall never know whether John is being serious.

Of Sir Richard Colt Hoare I cannot speak highly enough for he has entertained this callow youth and given sanctuary and encouragement to my own investigations and I one day promise to contribute to his great library with my own modest work;

"Manufactured flint tools and their essential use in everyday life before the common availability of metal by the ancient people of South Wiltshire with an investigation into the likely sources of flint of the finest quality."

I am perhaps a fool to value the ubiquitous flint above the allure of precious gold but it is my conviction that flint has enabled ancient man to survive and prosper for countless millennia whilst gold is a most divisive and corrupting material. Indeed it is not the fault of gold for every species upon this earth has been content to leave it untroubled amongst the streambeds or in its buried seams and it is only mankind that have become enslaved to this rare and beautiful metal.

Please do as you like with this correspondence and indeed John informs me that he collected all my remaining letters from my wretched uncle's abode. I have no use for them.

Your faithful and most grateful friend,
HENRY CHALK
or, if you should prefer,
A PEDESTRIAN.

POSTSCRIPT

Sir, I have this evening received news of the fate of my uncle James Chalk. Mr Gerrity, our brewery manager, arrived with correspondence from his twin brother who crossed the Atlantic five years ago and has a printing business in Philadelphia. There is a cutting before me upon the desk from the "Philadelphia Aurora" newspaper reporting "The execution of an Englishman" and informs of events that occurred now five weeks ago. In summary, the man was tried and convicted for the stealing of a horse and saddle and upon the scaffold he declared that his name was not as he had previously given; Robert Foster of Minehead, England, but instead; James David Chalk of Southwark, London. The felon concluded that he could not depart from this world bearing a false name and he deeply regretted the course that his life had taken and he now implored the hangman to be swift about his work. The hangman duly complied and at half past ten o clock on the morning of Wednesday April 26th 1809 the Englishman James David Chalk was executed.

The pen shakes in my hand and of a sudden I am a child

once more. There have been days when I have convinced
myself that my uncle's evil deeds were a consequence of
an illness, indeed a malign tumour that did grow and grow
until all goodness was forced aside by an all consuming
and parasitic evil.

I am left to contemplate the wreckage of the Chalk
family and try as I might to piece together these broken
fragments I am now denied a confession from my uncle as
to the full extent of the evil deeds that he has orchestrated.
After our flight to Exeter my uncle was close upon our coat
tails and whilst our backs were turned he removed his
trunk and remaining belongings and fled. His whereabouts
have been the subject of much speculation but tonight I
have learned that he sought refuge in Philadelphia and
after committing further crimes was caught and did pay the
ultimate price. That he used the name of my dear friend
Robert Foster makes my skin crawl for to take a good man's
name and to only confess to this deceit upon the scaffold
indeed confirms the unscrupulous nature of my uncle.

As a consequence of this news I have forfeited a night
at the theatre and I did send word immediately to Robert
and Sarah Foster that circumstances had determined
that regrettably I could not attend. I hope that I have not
spoiled their pleasure this evening but my world is again
turned upon its head.

I would be gratified if you could communicate the
news of my wretched uncle's demise to our mutual friends

for none have been spared the anguish of these last few months.

When I read again, as I have just now done, the page written in my father's hand that tells of an unscheduled visit to Silbury Hill in May 1782 by two young brothers I cannot see the man that my uncle became, nor foretell that he would one day take the life of his elder brother.

As I look up from this page I see Mr Shorto's beautiful illustration of the red admiral butterfly upon my desk and it warms my heart. My dear Mr Fenton, I shall forever treasure the memories of my mother and my father and of late in my dreams they appear as a young and happy couple for that was surely their condition before my accursed uncle preyed upon their lives.

As I conclude this postscript the door bell rings and my heart races for I can now hear Robert and Sarah in the hallway talking with the housekeeper Mrs Harrison and on my account they have forfeited an evening at the theatre.

Sir, in so many ways, I am a very fortunate man.

The Coded Message

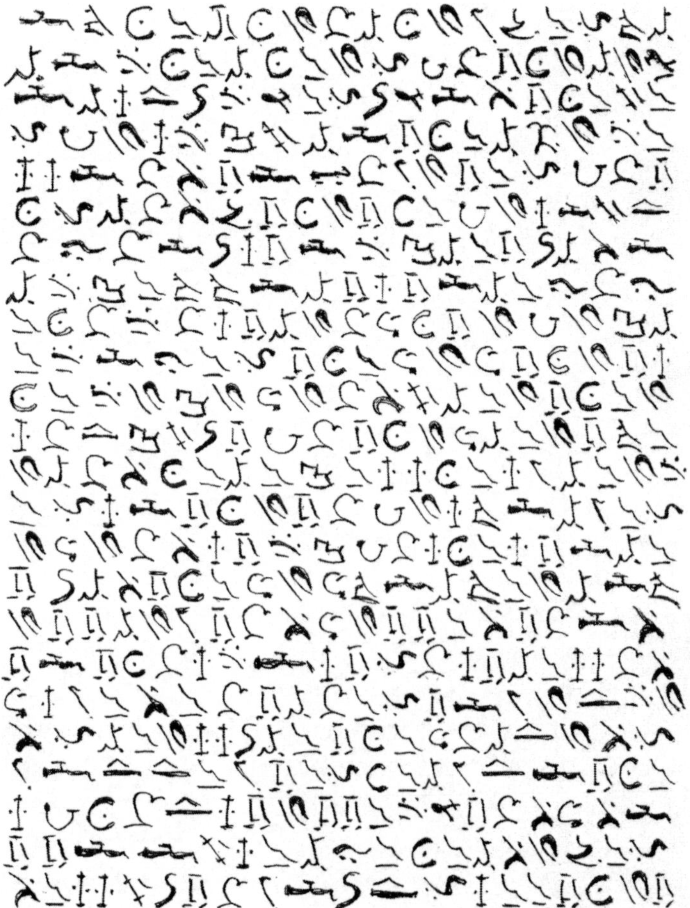

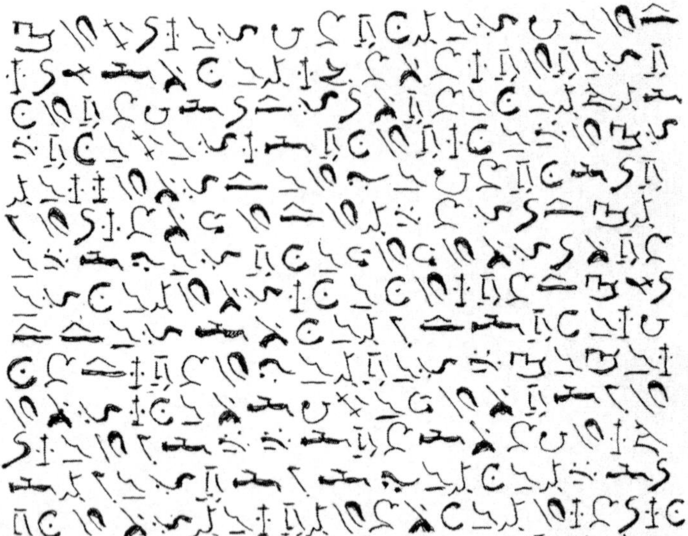

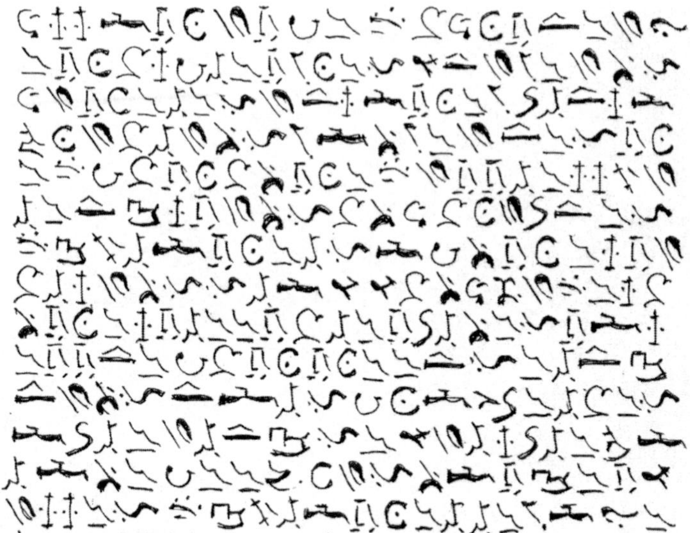